THE NAME OF THE FLOWER

OTHER TITLES IN
THE ROCK SPRING COLLECTION
OF JAPANESE LITERATURE

Death March on Mount Hakkoda by Jiro Nitta
Wind and Stone by Masaaki Tachihara
Still Life by Junzo Shono
Right under the big sky, I don't wear a hat by Hosai Ozaki

The Name of the Flower

STORIES BY
KUNIKO MUKODA

translated from the Japanese by Tomone Matsumoto

STONE BRIDGE PRESS
Berkeley, California

Published by STONE BRIDGE PRESS
P.O. Box 8208, Berkeley, CA 94707

Library of Congress Cataloging-in-Publication Data

Mukoda, Kuniko, 1929–1981
  *The Name of the flower : stories / by Kuniko Mukoda; translated
from the Japanese by Tomone Matsumoto.—1st ed.*
    p.   cm.
  *Translation of 13 stories selected from "Omoide toranpu" and
"Odoki, medoki."*
  ISBN 1-880656-09-4.
  1. Mukoda, Kuniko, 1929–1981   —Translations into English.
PL856.U65A26   1993
895.6'35—dc20   93-6309
                                                    CIP

Contents

The Name of the Flower

WHEN TSUNEKO PLACED A SMALL CUSHION MADE FROM LEFT-over scraps of material beneath the telephone, Matsuo, her husband, protested. "What's this for? I grew up without a cushion to sit on!" If a man could do without a cushion, then so could a telephone, he implied.

Tsuneko was about to reply that without the cushion the bell made a loud, irritating noise, but she managed to bite her lip. Any negative comments were taboo in Matsuo's presence for fear he would take them as a personal attack. Instead, Tsuneko laughed and defended herself, declaring that since she had felt the chill in her lower limbs and hips for the first time that winter, when she saw the bare telephone sitting on the shiny, white-enamel table she had realized it suffered from a cold bottom as well! Matsuo didn't press the matter further but went into their bedroom, rubbing his back with a towel. He was nearing fifty, and his back appeared much broader now than it used to. The droplets of water glistened on his skin, giving it a certain luster.

He had not been like this when he was young. Then, when he was losing ground in some petty squabble with Tsuneko, he would shrug his narrow, bony shoulders, turn his back on her, and march into the bedroom. On such occasions, his back seemed to say, "So what about it?" In bed, he would reach out for her without fail, as if trying to prove something to her before the next morning. Crushed by his weight, Tsuneko used to think he was attempting to even the score. Without a word, he would suddenly force himself on her in the dark. After ejaculating, he immediately fell asleep.

But this didn't happen anymore. In five minutes now, she would hear him snoring. Twenty-five years had thickened his body, and now, after giving his opinions on family and household matters, he left the routine business to her. Tsuneko could hear the midnight playing of the national anthem from the television next door. The neighbors always waited until after the anthem had been played to turn off the television.

Tsuneko's son and daughter, both university students, were not yet home; she didn't know where they were or what they were doing. The fact that she thought the sound of the telephone ringing was sharp enough to warrant a cushion indicated how much time Tsuneko spent by herself, waiting for the family to come home—with the four of them at home having tea, she didn't hear the national anthem at all.

Tsuneko realized that ever since she had installed the cushion she looked forward to the telephone ringing. The sharp bell had become mellow, and she wanted to hear the difference. Moreover, every time the phone rang lately, it brought good news: her son got a job; her husband was promoted to head of finance; the manager of the supermarket told her that the money was gone but the purse itself (her late mother's keepsake), which she had dropped while shopping, had been found. All this good news was conveyed by the mild ringing of the telephone.

Tsuneko peeled some potatoes. Some old ones, the previous year's crop, were sprouting. Scooping out the sprouts, she recalled the first time her mother had shown her how to hold the knife. "Potato sprouts are poisonous," she'd said. She had also told Tsuneko that she could die if she ate potatoes with peppermints. Tsuneko wondered how old she had been when, while eating curry and rice or potato croquettes, she had suddenly recalled eating peppermints earlier in the day and was terrified she was going to die.

The bell rang in the dining room. Tsuneko was pleased with its soft tone; picking up the telephone, she answered in a happy voice.

When she gave her surname, a voice asked, "Are you the lady of the house?" It was a woman's voice she had not heard before.

"Who's calling, please?" Tsuneko asked.

After a long pause, the voice replied, "I know your husband well."

It was Tsuneko's turn to be silent. "It couldn't be" and "Just as I thought"—the two emotions whirled around in her head like a blue-and-red-striped barber's pole turning in front of a shop.

The woman said she wanted to meet Tsuneko sometime during the day to talk privately about her husband. Tsuneko heard the woman's words as if they were meant for someone else. At the other end of the taut, black telephone cord a woman was sitting alone in the darkness. Neither her face nor her figure could be seen but, like Tsuneko, she sat holding a telephone receiver. She could be half Tsuneko's age or slightly older. She didn't sound like a housewife; she probably worked in a bar. Fumbling with the ornamental red silk tassels that dangled from the four corners of the small telephone cushion, Tsuneko noticed that they were soiled. She wondered how they had gotten dirty so quickly; it was less than a month since she had put the cushion under the telephone.

She arranged to meet the woman in a hotel lobby early that evening.

"How will I recognize you?" Tsuneko asked.

"I'll know you." The woman laughed softly.

How could she know me, Tsuneko wondered. Had Matsuo shown her a family photo? Tsuneko realized her underarms were clammy with perspiration. She asked the woman her name and she fell silent, thinking she heard "Tsuneko." So, my husband has a mistress with the same name as me, she thought, but soon realized her mistake—the woman's name was Tsuwako.

The woman repeated her name: "Tsuwako. 'Tsuwa,' as in the flower *tsuwabuki*, the silverleaf."

"Are those the stone and butterbur characters?"

"No, you just write the sounds, Tsu-wa-ko, in *hiragana*," the woman said.

Tsuneko remained seated for a while. The black receiver was stained with white fingerprints from the potato starch. Suddenly, the whole thing seemed to be a huge joke; she bent over in laughter when she remembered that the woman's name was the name of a flower.

On their first date after they had been introduced as potential marriage partners, Tsuneko found that Matsuo knew only the names for cherry blossoms, chrysanthemums, and lilies. But when Tsuneko asked him to describe these flowers, his confidence faltered. "I'm certain about the cherry blossom because it was my junior high school symbol," he said. When Tsuneko asked him the difference between a cherry blossom and a plum blossom, he couldn't reply.

Matsuo's ignorance was probably not limited just to the names of flowers, or so suspected Tsuneko. "I don't think I'll marry him," she had sighed when she got home. It was a dismal prospect for the twenty-year-old woman to contemplate, spending the rest of her life with a man so indifferent to the details of daily life. Tsuneko's mother, however, after hearing her daughter's declaration, suddenly became anxious for her to marry Matsuo. A man like that would make any woman happy, she claimed. "Look at your father," she said.

Tsuneko's father was a connoisseur in one way, but he really didn't excel at anything. When presented with a fish, he could make beautiful sashimi; he could wrap and decorate parcels far better than his wife; he knew what kimono best suited a woman and could skillfully select the right pattern. He knew how to please a woman—unknown to Tsuneko, he had had several affairs—but he hadn't advanced very far in his career as a public servant.

When Tsuneko met Matsuo again after her mother's urging, he murmured, "I'm a social dimwit." Tsuneko looked up at this man who was a head taller than she. He told her that he had grown up being told by his parents that he would go to a famous school and be first in his class. He only cared for mathematics and economics. He raced through life, always looking ahead. "If we get married," he said, "promise me you'll take lessons in flower arrangement and then teach me how."

Tsuneko had nearly flung herself on him with joy, but she controlled herself, thinking that would not be ladylike. But soon Matsuo stretched out his bony hand to hold hers.

If you like, I'll teach you everything I know; the names of flowers, fish, and vegetables, said Tsuneko to herself.

Matsuo was as good as his word. When he and Tsuneko returned from their honeymoon, he found a nearby flower arrangement teacher. Once a week Tsuneko had a lesson, and on those days Matsuo would come straight home from work. He quickly finished his dinner and then had Tsuneko arrange the flowers as she had learned that day. He watched her closely, like a surgeon given a precious opportunity to observe an important operation. "What's the name of that flower?" he would always ask. Without fail, every night after a flower arrangement lesson, Matsuo's lovemaking would be rough and brutal. This was the routine for years.

In the fifth year of their marriage, Tsuneko happened by chance to see Matsuo's notebook. On the days of her lessons, Matsuo had written the names of the flowers he'd learned from her:

March 15: Daffodil (yellow)
March 22: Spirea (white)

Furthermore, at the end of each line, the word "Done" was written and circled. When Tsuneko checked further back in the notes, the mark was there almost without exception.

She recalled one of those lesson days. Matsuo had come home in good humor. He had been invited to his superior's home and he alone among the guests had been able to identify the rare flowers arranged by his superior's wife and placed in the alcove. The superior and his wife were most impressed. Matsuo repeated the story to Tsuneko, then sat down formally and bowed deeply, saying, "It was all your doing." It was the first time she'd seen her husband enraptured by a compliment from his superior. It was true she was slightly disappointed in his boast, a side of him she hadn't known before, but his words, "Thanks to you, I've become human," flattered her and she didn't feel bad about it. Besides, Tsuneko looked forward to his rough manner in bed, too. She was unsure whether his behavior that night was responsible, but soon after she suffered a miscarriage. Had the baby been born, it would have been their third child.

After this incident, the pattern of her teaching him the minutiae of daily life, and he responding with lessons in bed, became less constant. Matsuo was a genuine and honest man, and it was possible that he had taken her miscarriage to heart. There was no longer any need to teach him the difference between bass and gray mullet, Spanish mackerel and butterfish, spinach and Chinese cabbage, basil and parsley. He had learned to do it himself. He also began to learn the different breeds of dogs—Akita, Tosa, Shiba, German Shepherd, Great Dane, and so on.

But old customs die hard. Tsuneko still wanted Matsuo to repeat back what she had taught him.

"Oh, shut up!" Matsuo exclaimed, "I know that!" But then he added, "The Siamese is the one that looks like a fox and the Persian looks like a raccoon dog. Right?"

"No. It's the other way round," Tsuneko corrected him.

In life's little details, Tsuneko was still the teacher. If she let him, he would keep wearing the same suit, perspiring in a heavy winter fabric in the spring. Things hadn't changed in twenty-five years. He would wear the underwear Tsuneko took from the chest of drawers for him. "I don't understand color coordination," he would say, taking a necktie from Tsuneko's hand. On social occasions, funerals and parties, as well as at the weddings of subordinates, he would give the speeches Tsuneko had prepared for him. His daughter jokingly said that he would be hopeless without her mother to look after him. And on the whole, he was an unremarkable father to his children.

Matsuo did well at work and was promoted before his coworkers, and because he was so serious, so honest, and so hardworking, Tsuneko somehow thought he would never betray her with another woman. But he did have a woman, and she had the name of a flower. Perhaps Matsuo had been attracted to her because of the name, Tsuneko thought. "So my lessons have begun to bear fruit now," she muttered. She laughed aloud once again, but it was a forced laugh. "What's the matter with you, Mom?" her daughter asked, coming home to pick up her tennis racket. But it wasn't something she could tell her daughter.

Tsuneko had no time to go to the beauty parlor to have her hair done before she went to see the woman, but she was able to finish peeling the potatoes. She found herself hollowing out large chunks of pale pink sprouts.

The woman who called herself Tsuwako was in her early thirties and looked like a mama-san at a second-class bar. Her kimono and her make-up were subdued and discreet, not at all cheap. On her way to the hotel, Tsuneko had speculated on why the woman wanted to meet her—was she pregnant, did she want money, or was it something even more serious? Unable to guess, she decided to wait and see. When Tsuneko discovered the woman had wanted to see her for no particular reason, she was slightly disappointed. Asked the purpose of the meeting, the woman, fondling the handle of her coffee cup, said, "I just wanted you to know about my relationship with your husband." Falling silent, she gazed at the artificial waterfall in the hotel garden.

Breaking the silence, which had become unbearable, Tsuneko told the woman that she and Matsuo had celebrated their silver wedding anniversary the previous year, that her grown-up children were facing important milestones in their lives—getting a job and marriage—and that although she was unaware of her husband's relationships outside their home, she had no intention of breaking up the family. And so on.

Tsuwako was silent.

"Yours is a very unusual name, Tsuwako. Did my husband tell you as soon as he heard it that it was the name of a flower?" Tsuneko asked. If she had said yes, Tsuneko was ready to tell the woman about the old days when she had taught Matsuo the names of the flowers.

But it wasn't so.

"No, he didn't," Tsuwako said slowly. "Well, come to think of it, he did ask me later if my name, Tsuwako, was taken from *tsuwari*, for morning sickness." Tsuwako smiled good-naturedly. "No parents would name their child after morning sickness, would they?" Then she added a surprising comment: at Tsuwako's bar, Matsuo referred to his wife as "my teacher."

"'My teacher?'"

"I understand you're very clever. You're not like me. Everyone thinks I'm a fool," said Tsuwako.

Tsuneko noticed how Tsuwako was wearing her kimono loosely; she talked slowly and stirred her coffee slowly. Perhaps she is a bit of a fool as she says, but if she is pretending, then she is the worst sort of woman, Tsuneko thought. Tsuneko, who was now supposed to know everything, paid for her coffee and came home none the wiser.

That night Matsuo and her children were all out late. Sitting in the dining room by herself, waiting for the family to return home, she felt anger boiling up inside her. "I'm a social dimwit," "Please teach me," "Thanks to you"—these past fragments of conversation flashed through her mind. What were they, after all? What had made him put those marks in his datebook at the end of every lesson? Tsuneko wondered.

Matsuo arrived home as usual. Tsuneko bit back the words she wanted to throw at him, casually asking, "Do you know the Japanese silverleaf?"

"Japanese silverleaf?" Matsuo repeated, his breath smelling of sake. "Is that the one with yellow flowers?"

"Do you know a woman called Tsuwako, the silverleaf?"

"Haven't seen that flower lately," he said.

"There was a phone call from her today," Tsuneko called out, as he walked away from her toward their bedroom. "Why on earth—"

Matsuo stopped, his back still to her. "That's over. All over," he said and went into the room. His back, broader than ever, seemed to say, "What about it?"

Tsuneko had put herself up on a pedestal because she had taught him the flowers' names and had been useful to him. True, she had nurtured him in the old days, but the young sapling had now grown into a big tree without her realizing it.

The name of the flower? What about it?

The name of the woman? What about it?

That's what her husband's back seemed to say.

The woman had stood still, but the man had graduated, increasing the gap between them.

Tsuneko heard the national anthem on the television next door.

Small Change

IT HAD BEEN AGREED THAT SHOJI WOULD GIVE THREE DOU-
ble knocks on the door and that the door plate would not have
his name on it. The security window, covered by a curtain, was
rectangular and wide enough for visitors to be identified at the
door. When Shoji gave the agreed knock, the curtain was raised
and Tomiko's eyes appeared. It had been a year since Shoji had
taken Tomiko as his mistress, but every time he looked at her
eyes he couldn't help thinking how small they were. They were
like the cracks on a chapped hand, and when she smiled, the
cracks seemed to split open.

It was only in the last month or so that Tomiko had started
to smile at him through the window.

"You do like me coming, don't you?" Shoji once asked.

Tomiko slowly nodded her head.

"Then why don't you smile at me?"

Since then, the taciturn, clumsy Tomiko had taken to smiling hesitantly when he came. Smiles didn't come easily to her
plain, flat face.

When she opened the door to greet Shoji, her sweaty body
silently leaned toward him, like a large tree falling to the ground.
This, too, was what Shoji had asked her to do. Before, she had
just stood at the door looking puzzled. She was twenty years old,

fair complexioned, with a sturdy figure. She had heeded Shoji's request not to wear make-up or perm her hair.

As she leaned toward him, Tomiko opened her hand. Inside was a ping-pong ball.

"Ah." Shoji immediately understood what this was about. He had only managed to visit her once the previous week. Sitting on the tatami floor sipping a glass of cold barley tea, he had remarked that the floor wasn't level, maybe because the apartment house was built on a slope. He wanted to test his theory and asked her if she had anything that would roll. Tomiko didn't, but apparently she had remembered his request.

"Did you buy this?" Shoji asked her.

"A hundred and twenty yen," she replied, as if apologizing for the price, and placed the ball on the tatami floor.

The ball did not roll. Shining in the direct rays of the western sun, the white ping-pong ball just remained where it was. This was Tomiko herself, thought Shoji. She would do nothing unless she was told, but she was obedient. That was precisely why he was keeping her as his mistress. Shoji had just turned fifty.

He visited Tomiko twice a week, always getting out of the taxi at the bottom of the hill. It was a one-way street heading down, but even if it hadn't been Shoji would have stopped the taxi and got out. The taxi meter was just about to go up. Although he was a successful man—he owned a small company and had a chauffeur-driven car—he couldn't help watching the meter. Whenever a taxi approached his destination and the meter was about to go up, he would tell the driver to stop, saying, "This'll do," and scurry along the rest of the way. He felt like laughing at himself. No wonder he was nicknamed Mouse.

The only time Shoji wasn't in a hurry was when he went to Tomiko's apartment. When he got out of the taxi, he would buy a pack of cigarettes at the tobacco shop on the corner and then slowly climb the hill. The slope wasn't steep enough to stop him from walking at his usual brisk pace, but he wanted to walk slowly. He had a kept woman in a two-room apartment. It wasn't a brand new apartment, and the woman wasn't a beauty he could proudly take out in public, but keeping a woman gave him a certain status. There was a bounce of anticipation in his step. The word *hanamichi* kept flickering in his mind. Man's procession to the stage, the way to the top. Walk slowly and proudly onto the stage, he thought.

The neighborhood where Tomiko lived was an upper-class residential area, formerly part of the Azabu district. On both sides of the road were old houses or newly rebuilt ones, all with spacious gardens. One house had a high stone wall covered with ivy. White magnolia, wisteria, yellow roses, crepe myrtle, and other flowers blossomed in the gardens of the houses along the hill. Shoji walked slowly, peeping through the hedges at the gardens. Breathing in the sweet fragrance of daphne, Shoji realized that he hadn't smelled that scent for many years.

As he looked at the flowers and plants, Shoji recalled that it had been cherry blossom time last year when he had found the apartment for Tomiko. The cherry tree standing halfway up the hill had been spreading its petals all over the road; looking at the large tree now with its dark green leaves, he could hardly believe it had shed so many blossoms.

Tomiko had been one of several young women who had applied for a clerk's position in Shoji's company. She was on the short list for an interview because she could handle an abacus and her calligraphy was excellent. But she was the very first to be dropped from the final selection.

"This one's quite hopeless," said the personnel manager, just after Tomiko had bowed and left the room. "She's too big,"

he added, as if to ingratiate himself with Shoji, who was small
for a man.

"She's dumb. You can tell by her thick ankles," the head of
accounting chimed in, scrawling "No good" on the assessment
sheet.

"*Mennai chidori no takashimada*," the personnel manager
began to sing, mocking Tomiko's narrow eyes. "An eyeless bird
in a wedding dress."

"That's an old song!" they all said, laughing.

Their remarks about Tomiko were all true; she was too tall
and too heavy. She looked unhappy, with her narrow eyes and
expressionless face. Her clothes were old-fashioned and her
responses to the interview questions dull. Her high school
record was below average, and she had no outstanding relatives
in her family.

"Can't imagine a girl like that still exists." Shoji, too, marked
"No good" on the sheet, but he stealthily made a note of
Tomiko Kadowaki's name and address. His hand seemed to
move of its own accord.

Tomiko had been born in the Shakotan Peninsula in
Hokkaido. It was quite some time before she began to talk to
Shoji about her upbringing. When she talked about her early
years, she told him that beef (Hokkaido was cattle country) was
rarely on the table when she was growing up—meat, for her,
meant horsemeat. For whatever reason, innovations such as plastic food wrap had bypassed her village. Men who had left and
gone to Tokyo to earn extra money would return—perhaps for a
funeral—and ask why the village had none of this handy wrap to
store cooked vegetables in the refrigerator. They tried to explain
exactly what the plastic wrap looked like, but the women

couldn't imagine it at all; they had never seen it. Shoji laughed heartily when Tomiko told him this.

When Tomiko took off her clothes, her white body appeared larger than ever. She reminded Shoji of a New Year's Day rice-cake, large and shiny, and he was the mouse who climbed up and played upon it.

"Perhaps your grandmother or great-grandmother had an affair with a Russian, eh?" Shoji asked her once, half-joking but half-serious.

"Well, who knows?" Tomiko cocked her head to one side.

On such occasions, her narrow eyes betrayed no emotions. Shoji couldn't tell whether she was happy or angry.

Tomiko had wept when she had yielded to him that first time, in the hotel. Tears had welled up in her eyes, like a swollen stream. These were not the delicate, pearl-like tear-drops he had seen depicted in paintings; obviously, such tears didn't fall from tiny, half-closed eyes.

Tomiko wasn't the sort of "sensitive" girl who would jump to anticipate Shoji's every need. That was precisely what Shoji liked about her. He could relax. In her room, he didn't have to put on an act or be status-conscious. After a bath, he could sit crosslegged with a towel around his waist and sip his beer with boiled baby beans and chilled tofu. Or he could eat a thin pork cutlet bought from a nearby shop, smothering it with Worcester-shire sauce. He could read page three of the newspaper first instead of the front page. No one said anything. There was no son or daughter to make faces when he pronounced English words such as "the PTA" or "dance party" in his Japanese way.

Shoji was a self-made man. After elementary school, he had entered a five-year vocational program at an electrical and com-munications school, and he had worked his way up to where he was now. In Tomiko's room he didn't have to put up with a wife who belonged to all kinds of social clubs—a tea ceremony club, a cooking club—and spent hours holding affected conversations with her club friends on the telephone.

Shoji appreciated Tomiko's frugality. She disliked waste and didn't turn on the lights until it was quite dark. Once, when Shoji was eating a slice of watermelon, she had taken it from him, saying it was watery when it was guaranteed to be sweet, and returned it to the fruit shop at the foot of the hill. "It wasn't as sweet as you said," she declared and stood there, staring at the shop owner with her inscrutable eyes—or so Shoji had imagined. Shoji saw the funny side of it all, and began to feel an affection for the Shakotan Peninsula. He thought he would arrange to take three or four days off and go to Hokkaido with Tomiko. They would have fun.

The only time Shoji and Tomiko had an argument was when he discovered that Tomiko was doing some accounting work for the woman in the next apartment. The woman, Umezawa, was the mama-san in a nearby bar. Shoji knew her face. Several times he had encountered her halfway up the hill. Once, when he'd seen her in front of the apartment as she was putting out the garbage, she had bowed to him as if she knew about his relationship with Tomiko.

Umezawa was thirty-five or thirty-six, an attractive woman with Western features—the kind of face that would never have been seen in Japan in the old days. Shoji had told Tomiko not to socialize with her neighbors in the apartment building, but at some point she had asked Umezawa how to use the gas hot water system, and the two had struck up an acquaintance. Tomiko told Shoji that she wasn't helping Umezawa for the money—she did the work because she had nothing to do all day.

A strange force seemed to emanate from Tomiko's big, white body as she said this.

About the end of summer, Shoji took a trip to Bangkok and Singapore for ten days—part business, part vacation. He had several opportunities to choose a dark-skinned and small-boned, lithe body in these places, but he returned to Japan without doing so. Away in those countries where everything was the color of chocolate—the mountains, the water, the people—Shoji missed the large white lump that was Tomiko in Tokyo. He wanted to eat chilled tofu or boiled beans with a towel around his waist, sitting on the tatami that glowed red in the sunlight from the western sky.

Shoji returned to Tokyo one day ahead of schedule. He had never stayed with Tomiko all night, but he wanted to that day. As a souvenir, he had bought Tomiko a sapphire—though not an expensive one.

I'll surprise her by knocking on the door without calling her first, he thought. I wonder how she'll react when she looks out the window slit and finds me outside. Shoji kept anticipating the situation; it made him feel younger.

Arriving at the foot of the hill as usual, Shoji bought a pack of cigarettes. He had plenty of cigarettes in Tomiko's room, but he found himself falling back into his usual habit, knocking on the glass window of the tobacco shop. This ritual signaled the beginning of his secret life, just like the sound of wooden clappers before the curtain rises in the Kabuki theater. Shoji usually carried some small change, but on that day he had run out. While the old woman at the tobacco shop went to get change, Shoji looked around and caught a glimpse of his face in a small mirror inside the shop. He looked very much like his late father. Perhaps it was his inheritance to look shriveled as he grew older—and to look like a mouse. Oh, well, he thought to himself, even a mouse has times when his blood is on fire!

When Shoji was in the fifth grade, his father, a carpenter, had taken him to see a Korean dancer named Choe Sung-hui. He didn't remember how his father had obtained the tickets. Did he buy them, or had someone given them to him? He remembered more vividly that his mother, pregnant with his youngest sister, had bought him a pack of caramels and put it in the pocket of his school uniform. He also clearly recalled the figure of Choe Sung-hui dancing on the stage, beating a large Korean drum. The colors of her costume were unlike any a Japanese dancer would wear, and her fat white body shone with perspiration. The rhythm and beat of the drum became faster and more frenzied and the dancer seemed to Shoji to be wearing nothing at all. Suddenly she collapsed on the stage, and the packed hall shook with applause.

Shoji was surprised to notice that his father, sitting next to him, was clapping louder than anyone else. His father had always seemed so submissive to Shoji's mother. His only hobby was playing Japanese chess. Shoji hadn't seen this side of the man before—on the edge of his seat, his mouth hanging open, clapping with all his might. Shoji sensed that he shouldn't tell his mother about this different father.

Now, reflected in the shop's small mirror, was the face of a man going to see a woman young enough to be his daughter, the face of his father watching the dancer. And Choe Sung-hui also had had a large white body with a thick waist.

Shoji knocked on the door as usual, but the curtain over the peephole didn't open. Tomiko couldn't be out, because he had heard the sound of the toilet flushing inside the apartment just before he knocked. Shoji tapped at the door once again, but no response came from inside. There was no sound, but he knew someone was there behind the door. What was the matter? Nothing like this had happened before.

The door of the neighboring apartment opened and Umezawa peeped out. Her heavily made up face froze when she saw him, and she groped for words. Tomiko had a man inside! And this woman knew about it!

"Tomiko! Tomiko!" Shoji called loudly. He pummeled the door, abandoning the arranged knocking signal. At last the curtain over the peephole lifted from inside. What he saw was not Tomiko's eyes, but a pair of sunglasses. Was Tomiko's man a yakuza? Shoji's heart began to thump.

But he was wrong. There was no man inside the apartment. It was Tomiko wearing the dark glasses. Her eyes were swollen and reddish purple. She reminded him of Oiwa, the disfigured heroine in a village Kabuki play he had once seen. While Shoji had been away in Bangkok, Tomiko had had surgery on both her eyelids. Umezawa had arranged it all.

"Why did you do that without telling me?" Shoji gave Tomiko a gentle push. This must have dislodged the ping-pong ball, because it fell lightly down onto the floor from behind the clock on the chest of drawers; it bounced a few times on the tatami and rolled slowly toward a corner of the room.

I liked your eyes the way they were, Shoji thought; those eyes like the splits on my mother's hands. They opened when you smiled; when you cried they brimmed over with tears. I liked those eyes of yours.

Tomiko sat motionless in her dark glasses. Shoji couldn't tell what she was thinking. The dark glasses made it harder than ever to read her thoughts. Tomiko was wearing a Hawaiian muu-muu, and her bare back glowed with the western sun behind it. Shoji noticed a pale pink polish on her fingernails. He thought she was a little slimmer. Tomiko said not a word of apology about her eyes.

After ten days had passed and the swelling had subsided, Tomiko's eyes looked just like those of her next-door neighbor. Well, not exactly the same—each person's eyes are different— but when the same doctor performs the operation the results can be similar, or so Shoji had heard. Tomiko began to talk a lot more now. Both her face and body became more expressive. Every day she appeared to have more confidence. The more her self-esteem increased, the more exhausted Shoji felt.

He had never disliked the gentle slope before, but on this particular day he was reluctant to climb it. He found himself telling the taxi driver to take a different route, and he got off at the top of the hill. He wondered why it had never occurred to him to walk down the hill, discarding the petty idea of saving seventy yen or so. It was easy to walk down the mild incline— he passed different hedges and gardens and nameplates, not the same old ones he saw when he climbed up from the bottom of the hill.

Tomiko might not open the door when I knock, he thought. Next she'll fix her nose, then her cheeks, and gradually she'll look exactly like the woman next door. Her white, cylindrical, shapeless body will have a trim waist and slim ankles. He fanta-sized that he was sleeping on a large, white ricecake offered up to a deity, only to find it had turned into a white mannequin. To be honest, Shoji's regret was mixed with relief.

He had never realized before how high up this small hill was relative to the rest of Tokyo. As he glanced down, he had a good view of a shopping center. The roofs, the windows, the sign-boards, all had an orange glow in the setting sun. Shoji had been climbing up and down this hill for a year, but the sun had always been at his back on his way up, and it was usually dark when he went home. Sometimes he was preoccupied with concocting excuses to explain his lateness to his wife. So he had never seen the area at sunset.

Shall I just keep on walking down this hill, Shoji thought, without dropping in at Tomiko's apartment? Shall I buy a pack of cigarettes at the tobacco shop at the bottom and get a taxi home? Halfway down, he stood still and fumbled in his pocket for change.

I Doubt It

I CAN'T LEAVE THE SICKROOM.

Shiozawa knew very well that he shouldn't leave the patient until someone came to take his place beside the bed. His father was asleep, his snores echoing in the private hospital room. He had collapsed from a cerebral hemorrhage three days ago, shortly after his seventy-seventh birthday, and had been unconscious ever since. It was his father's second stroke, and Shiozawa had just been told there was little chance of recovery—that he should prepare for the worst. Because his father's heart was still strong for his age, the critical time was expected to come between midnight and dawn. Shiozawa's wife had waited there impatiently for him to come from work, and was now home, ready to make preparations for the mourning clothes and the funeral.

All the others whom his father ought to see, Shiozawa thought, had said their goodbyes—not that there were many others. His father had been stiff and narrow-minded and had grown even more cantankerous after his wife died. When the first stroke had paralyzed him a year ago, his dislike of contact with others increased. The flowers and get-well gifts in the room were mere formalities, acknowledgments of the son's position as a company executive.

Outside, the sky turned gray and darkened at last. In the encroaching darkness, his father seemed to be fighting for a little more space in which to live. I'm his son. I've got to stay here by his bed, Shiozawa thought. But he found the room hard to bear. A stench rose from his father's mouth, which hung wide open, almost unhinged. The whiskers had kept growing after his collapse, and the mustache—an incongruous bundle of spindly twigs—trembled slightly with every breath. The heavy odor filled the room. Since it came from his parent, Shiozawa felt he should dutifully ignore it. But his father's smell was not just a sick man's bad breath. It was much more—the stink of rotting guts.

His father had always been a drudge, an elementary school principal who had continued working as an administrator long after his retirement. He was a social drinker, but never went too far. "Your father is the only man I know who never gets his shirt collar dirty," Shiozawa's mother had once remarked. Unlike his father, she at least would have an occasional evening drink of sake. She had insinuated that there was something lacking in a husband who, even as a young man, had so little sexual desire. Always thin, he looked in later life like a dried stick ready to be snapped in two. Passing him in a corridor, Shiozawa would think he resembled a cigarette holder, both in shape and smell.

What is this animal stink? Can't a man die without such a foul smell? Shiozawa had a hunch his father's time would be up earlier than the doctor had predicted. I can't leave my seat. The relatives all think I'm a good eldest son. So I won't take my eyes off him.

But the stench was unbearable. Shiozawa suspected that was why his wife had hurried out as soon as he came in. She couldn't take the smell either.

I've got to get a newspaper, Shiozawa decided. The evening papers would have arrived at the hospital kiosk. There had been stories recently about an acquaintance of Shiozawa's, an executive of an affiliated company who was suspected of bribery. Shiozawa knew it was just an excuse, but he left the room anyway.

When he returned with the fresh smell and smudge of newsprint on his hands, his father's snores had ceased. Shiozawa did not feel much grief. Pressing the buzzer to call the nurse, he wondered how he would explain to the relatives that he was not there at the end. His own odor was overpowering, and he pressed the button harder, noticing, as he did so, that the dead man's stench had disappeared completely, as if it had never been present.

Shiozawa's wife was phoning family members with information about the wake and the funeral arrangements. "What shall we do about Nobu-chan?" She looked up at him for an answer. Nobuo was Shiozawa's cousin.

"I don't think we need to tell him."

His wife came to Nobuo's defense. "But Nobu-chan doesn't seem to be in touch with anyone else in the family."

"He's not a child anymore. Why do you still call him 'Nobu-chan'?"

"He is twelve years younger than you, and—let's see—that makes him thirty-five."

"He's old enough to be respectable, but he hasn't settled down yet. That's why no one takes him seriously," Shiozawa rejoined.

"Not settled down"—it had been his father's favorite phrase. Every family had one or two black sheep, and Nobuo was theirs. He had formally enrolled at the university, but had soon quit. Since then, not once had he held a steady job; every time the family saw him, he had a different job and a different address.

Nobuo had once claimed to be a show business agent and had shown Shiozawa an album full of publicity pictures and photos of models in swimsuits. Shiozawa hadn't recognized even one of the "budding talents." Another time Nobuo had said he was an *anya*. Shiozawa thought that meant he ran a shop making the sweet bean filling for cakes, but Nobuo explained he was another kind of *anya*—a liaison between television broadcasters and manufacturers whose job it was to think up gimmicks for television commercials. For a commission, he had said.

Every time Nobuo changed his job, he changed his woman as well. Sometimes he appeared to be nothing more than a gigolo. Once he seemed quite poor; even his face looked strangely different. Then out of the blue he had sent Shiozawa a large box of prime canned crab as a year-end gift. Shiozawa's thank-you note came back stamped "Address unknown. Return to sender."

"That's true, but Grandfather was fond of him," Shiozawa's wife was saying.

"Go ahead and tell him then, if you want. I wouldn't," Shiozawa wanted to say. But he swallowed his words and began looking through a bundle of old New Year's greeting cards to find Nobuo's most recent address.

The women in the family all liked Nobuo. He was not particularly handsome, but he was subtly attractive and had a certain way about him. Shiozawa had noticed that when Nobuo walked into a room, it came alive. The women began to talk and laugh more.

Once—he didn't remember exactly when it was—his eldest daughter had returned from a friend's wedding and found

Nobuo talking with her mother in the dining room. Like her mother, his daughter was the thrifty type. She would normally take off her kimono after a social occasion so it would not get soiled. But this time she did not change until after Nobuo had left. She sat eating cakes and drinking tea in her best clothes. "What's the use of showing off for such a man?" Shiozawa wanted to ask her.

He noticed, however, that it wasn't just his daughter who acted that way. His wife, too, hovered attentively over the younger man. Apparently remembering a remark Nobuo had made many years ago, she offered him the choice bits of salted salmon: "You prefer the belly-meat, grilled medium, don't you Nobu-chan?" Shiozawa never heard such cheerful tones from his wife when they were alone together. It so happened that he liked that piece of the salmon himself, and he was outraged that his wife should offer the delicacy to Nobuo instead of to him. What's more, she enthusiastically listened to everything Nobuo said, occasionally nodding and stealing self-conscious glances at her own face reflected in the black lacquered tea caddy she was playing with, dabbing unobtrusively at her nose with her fingertips to remove the shine. Shiozawa did not fail to catch that.

"Whenever Nobu-chan's name comes up, you speak as if you hate him," Shiozawa's wife said.

"I don't mean to. I just don't want what happened before to happen again."

"Before? You mean what happened at the funeral?"

"That's right. I don't want any more money squabbles among the relatives," Shiozawa explained.

"But you didn't actually catch him at it."

"Who else would do such a thing?"

Two years before, at the funeral service for a member of the main branch of Shiozawa's family, a condolence gift of 50,000 yen had disappeared. Nobuo had been seen coming and going at about the time it happened. He had talked then as if he were doing well, but in fact he seemed broke. He had presented only a token gift—bundles of cheap incense in a splendid box. It was rumored that he had tried to borrow money from a rich widow in the family and had been refused. Shiozawa, who was in charge of the service, was mortified. He was determined to search Nobuo's belongings, but his wife and the other women talked him out of it. They didn't want a blood relative shamed in the presence of the deceased.

Shiozawa refused to let the matter drop. He made clear his suspicions to Nobuo himself, but the young man remained unperturbed. Adding insult to injury, he gathered the unmarried women and children around him and made a vulgar display, imitating chorus girls with his long, thin fingers. As Shiozawa watched the nicotine-stained, finely tapered fingers going up and down like dancers' legs, he thought it almost obscene. "Consider the occasion!" he wanted to object. It was all he could do to control himself.

Now he was chief mourner. Perhaps it was wrong to bask in this self-satisfied respectability, having just lost a father, but that was how he felt. The general-affairs section of his company came out in force and arranged the whole program—the ceremony at the funeral altar, the wake, and the ritual farewell to the deceased. It all reflected Shiozawa's position. Those relatives he was not ashamed of came, and his friends paid their condolence visits. He felt a twinge of guilt as he displayed the appropriate grief like an actor, but he told himself not to be concerned because every important occasion in life called for this kind of performance.

A huge lacquerware container of sushi was delivered to the

kitchen door from a large shop near the station. Shiozawa was told that whoever ordered the sushi had given no name but had simply told the shop where to deliver twenty servings of the best quality. Shiozawa and his wife glanced at each other: Nobuo. That was his way when he was in the money. Make people wonder, then put in an appearance. "This isn't a third-rate traveling theater production! Don't you try to upstage me!" Shiozawa planned to say. But then he noticed that the children had already started enjoying the sushi, and the opportunity was lost.

Nobuo turned up a little later.

"It'll be all right this time. He's wearing new shoes and a new suit," Shiozawa's wife whispered.

"Don't take your eyes off him. I can't afford to be shamed in front of the company's employees." Shiozawa raised his voice without realizing it, and his wife had to hush him.

Nobuo bowed to Shiozawa with a look and air he assumed especially on such occasions, and walked ceremoniously toward the funeral altar. He presented a condolence gift and politely offered incense. He sniffled noticeably as he pressed his palms together in prayer. It was more than Shiozawa could bear. When the eldest son of the deceased was not shedding tears, why should a distant relative give such a studied performance? Looking closely at Nobuo's black suit, he saw that the fabric was not an appropriately plain cloth; it had a small fish-scale weave. That truly irritated him. Shiozawa summed up the poseur to himself: Here is a man who gets along in the world by ingratiating himself and courting favors.

Nobuo came up to him to express his condolences. Shiozawa kept his eyes closed, inhaling the smell of incense and flowers. Every corner of the house is filled with the sweet smell of incense, even the bathroom and the pantry, he thought.

Suddenly there was a commotion at the entrance to the house. Whispers spread.

"The wife of Executive Director Kujiraoka has come."

"Former. The *former* Executive Director."

"Just 'Mrs. Kujiraoka' will do."

The voices interrupted and corrected one another.

Kujiraoka had died six months ago. He had lost his post the year before, handing it over in a sense to Shiozawa. Despair had driven him to a nervous breakdown, and his premature death was brought on by a combination of excessive drinking and sleeping pills. Shiozawa had presided at the funeral ceremonies. Now the widow, a frail figure, came to express her condolences and her renewed gratitude for the attentive way Shiozawa had managed things at that time. Compared with what he had done for her, she said, she could do nothing for him. She apologized and left quickly.

"Ku-ji-ra-o-ka." Just behind Shiozawa, Nobuo was muttering the name as if trying to remember something. To Shiozawa, the meaning was clear. After all, Nobuo was there, he thought. He heard me that night. Shiozawa felt a knife twisting in his back.

Shiozawa knew he had some small flaws. He would break the speed limit when the coast was clear. He would accept small illegal kickbacks if he felt absolutely sure he wouldn't be caught. More often than he cared to remember, he had indulged in safe little love affairs on business trips. Shiozawa disliked knowing that this other, shady side lived behind the facade of the reputable, respectable businessman, but he comforted himself: That's how we men are. Everyone does it some time or other.

Still, there was that one thing Shiozawa did not want to think about at all. He could not explain to himself why he had

done it. One summer evening when his wife and children were
at the theater, before he realized quite what he was doing, he
had picked up the phone and dialed the villa of the company
chairman. When the chairman's familiar hoarse voice came on
the line, Shiozawa had covered his mouth with a handkerchief
and whispered into the phone slanders about Kujiraoka—there
was a house he had built with illegal commissions and some
tawdry affairs with women. But when he had put down the
receiver after this one-sided conversation, Shiozawa sensed he
was not alone; someone else was in the house.

Nobuo was standing in the kitchen, drinking water.

"You should come through the front door when you visit
us!" Shiozawa could hear his own voice trembling.

"Are you home alone?" Nobuo's casual question was a relief.
But he had heard.

"I hear Nobu-chan brought 50,000 yen in condolence
money." Shiozawa's wife's voice came to him as if from a distance.

During the vigil in front of the altar, Shiozawa needled
Nobuo. The company employees had gone home, and only
close relatives remained. The wake was taking place on the second night, so most of them had fallen asleep from sheer exhaustion. The only ones left awake were Nobuo, Shiozawa, and his
wife, and even she occasionally nodded off.

Alcohol was making Shiozawa increasingly testy. "The
50,000 yen you offered is too much for a man of your status,
don't you think? Or are you trying to make up for something
you've done in the past?" He was of course referring to Nobuo's
embezzlement of the condolence money at the other family
funeral.

Nobuo just scratched his head and said, "I know I've caused

you trouble. I'll do what I can when I can," and he served Shiozawa more sake.

"I don't like a man who borrows a little money on Saturday, and conveniently forgets his debt the next day, just because it's a Sunday holiday. If he needs money, he should borrow it on Monday and borrow enough so he'll remember. You visit us only when you feel you're a big man and can pass around your engraved business cards."

Shiozawa had to make Nobuo angry. Only then would he know for sure whether his cousin had heard him slander Kujiraoka that night. "Where do you get off saying such a thing? Who do you think you are?" If only Nobuo would say something like that, Shiozawa would be free of this suffocating suspense. It was as if they were playing the card game I Doubt It. The cards had to be played in numerical order, and if a person suspected another player of putting down the wrong card, he could say, "I Doubt It!" If his challenge held up and it wasn't the right card, the challenger gained the point. But if the challenger was wrong, he took a big loss.

Shiozawa knew that if a single word about what he had done that night ever leaked out, his reputation would be destroyed; certainly his wife would despise him. But that would almost be a relief compared with this continual uncertainty about whether Nobuo had overheard the phone call. Shiozawa was calling "I Doubt It!" But Nobuo ignored his provocations, got himself drunk, and fell asleep.

Shiozawa's father had taught him how to play I Doubt It. Even as a child, Shiozawa had been good at guessing, and his less imaginative father was often tricked. When Shiozawa played the correct cards, his father would say "I Doubt It!" and lose the game.

One summer vacation, when Shiozawa was in the second or

third grade, his father had made him wait for an hour in the dimly lit Tachikawa Station in the western suburbs. He had taken the boy along to Okutama for some fishing, a rare treat, and on their way back home to the city, he had been stopped by a ticket taker. Shiozawa sat on a wooden bench alone, bitten by mosquitoes. After an interminable wait, his father emerged from the stationmasters's office. He suddenly looked very old.

His father had said nothing as they left the railway station. Then he had silently treated Shiozawa to a bowl of eel and rice. Shiozawa sensed that his father had played the wrong card. He had not paid the full fare and had been caught. Shiozawa also knew that he wasn't to tell his mother and younger brother and sister. But his father doubted him. Clearly he thought Shiozawa was one who told tales. Shiozawa suspected that was why, after that day, his father had never again opened his heart to him, and had never loved him as much as before.

Nobuo leaned against the altar dozing.

Could it be that he didn't hear me after all? Or is he just pretending? The carefree bum has me over a barrel. And there's not a damn thing I can do about it. Even if I call his bluff, I won't know the truth unless he turns his cards face up.

Shiozawa could not stop his thoughts.

He saw again before him his father's stooped figure as they walked together out of the railway station. Father, a man of reputation, of character, sullied himself that summer evening. And I, too. . . . The rotten stench at my father's deathbed is mine, too. Nobuo may have caught wind of the odor of my living decay.

All at once, abhorrence and nostalgia became as one. Shiozawa added some incense chips to the burner, which had almost gone out, and lit a new stick as well.

The Otter

IT WAS ON A MONDAY EVENING THAT THE CIGARETTE HAD slipped from his fingers. Takuji had been sitting on the wooden veranda and gazing out on the garden as he smoked. His wife, Atsuko, was folding the laundry in the tatami-matted room and chatting to him about their plans. The couple's opinions differed on what to do with their house, which stood on over six thousand square feet of property. Atsuko wanted to have the house demolished and build an apartment block—this was also the real estate agent's suggestion. Takuji, however, insisted that the change should come after his retirement, in three years. The house itself wasn't worth much, but the garden was another matter, since it had been left to him by his late father, an avid gardener. Takuji would come straight home from work, sit on the veranda, and gaze out on the garden as he puffed a cigarette. That was his daily routine.

A small stone carving crowned with five ringlets, and the plants, which reflected the changing seasons like a calendar, gradually faded as the darkness deepened into night. As he watched, Takuji felt the exhaustion of his hour and a half's commute drain away. The fact that his position as the head of the records section was a minor post and he was not set to climb far on the corporate ladder didn't worry him. His real place was on this veranda in this house, he felt. Atsuko seemed to sense his feelings and usually dropped the subject after a few comments, but on this day she argued her point of view.

"If you build an apartment block, I won't go to work," Takuji responded in a sharper voice than usual. At this moment the cigarette had slipped from his fingers as if a puff of wind was carrying it away from him. Was it windy? he wondered.

"Is there any breeze?" Takuji asked.

"Couldn't be. If there was, the wash would be dry by now," Atsuko said. She came out of the room onto the veranda, licked her index finger, and held it up in the air, rather like a candle. "No. No wind," she said.

Atsuko, nine years his junior, occasionally made childish gestures, perhaps because she was young at heart and also because they had no children. Her small, shiny black eyes like two watermelon seeds danced with enjoyment. Observing the fun in her eyes, Takuji didn't feel like mentioning the cigarette's fall. "Middle age. Numbness in hands and legs." Recalling the words of an advertisement for some medicine, though he couldn't remember the name of the company, he picked up the still smoking cigarette from the large flat rock where they placed their shoes. He felt as if he were wearing a glove.

Later, Takuji realized that this incident was the first symptom of his illness. He couldn't recall how many days had elapsed since he had dropped the cigarette, but suddenly at work he was unable to remember the name of the superior who was talking to him in front of his desk. It was either the same day or the next that he had returned home by taxi after having a few drinks with some colleagues. The moment he got out of the taxi he collapsed on the ground like a stringless puppet. The taxi driver helped him to stand up and he remained on his feet, but he realized the collapse was another symptom. A week after dropping the cigarette, Takuji had gone to the entrance hall to pick up the morning paper soon after waking up; returning to the dining room, he lost consciousness, clutching the frame of the shoji screen. He had suffered a mild stroke.

There were buzzing insects in Takuji's head. It had been a month since his fall, and the insects were making intermittent noises just at the base of his skull. Although he had only lost consciousness for about an hour, a slight paralysis remained. He could walk if he leaned on a stick, but his right hand couldn't hold chopsticks.

Atsuko was humming to herself. Since Takuji's fall, she had begun to hum more often. "Your illness isn't that bad. You'll soon get better. I'm not a bit depressed by it at all," her humming seemed to say. From the beginning she had been a naturally active person, but ever since Takuji's illness, when he had taken sick leave and stayed at home, she had become more active than ever. As she sat she shelled peas or crocheted; her hands and fingers were never still. When she had nothing to do, her eyes darted here and there.

Takuji heard someone at the front door. It sounded like a car salesman. Trying to follow their conversation, he expected Atsuko to say something like, "My husband is sick and we just can't afford to buy a new car." Listening intently to the conversation, he heard her say instead, "Sorry, my husband's in the car business," in her sing-song voice.

Yes. She would. That was her usual way of getting rid of salesmen. When it was cosmetics, her husband was in the cosmetics business, and when an encyclopedia salesman came to the door, he was in publishing. During their honeymoon period when a salesman came to sell blankets, she had told him in that same voice of hers, "My husband's in the textile business," glancing back at Takuji at the rear of the room and giving him a broad wink. Takuji thought he had married an interesting

woman and that she would never bore him. Indeed, she had
lived up to his expectations. As long as she worked hard and was
affectionate, he could turn a blind eye to her sing-song voice
telling fibs. Perhaps she was too good a wife for him. After all,
her fibs were harmless—and were for her and Takuji's benefit.

Atsuko opened the sliding door just enough to peep out.
Her smile was the same as it had been twenty years ago. Her
small, narrow nose turned up when she laughed; her wide-
set eyes seemed even farther apart, and she looked as if she
was making a joke. Takuji thought she resembled something,
but he couldn't recall precisely what it was. Irritably, he felt that
only half his brain was functioning. It was probably because of
his illness. At times like this, the insects in his head started
buzzing.

Atsuko was drinking red cream soda, blowing it through a
straw like a child so the red soda water and ice cream produced a
white foam. Her straw had a split, and red soda water flowed out
through the crack.

"Cut it out. Stop that," Takuji snapped. The next time, when
the veins burst in his head, it would be the end of him.

Takuji tried to scream but no sound came out. At that
moment, he was shaken awake. Was it a dream or was it real? He
wasn't sure which was which. He vaguely recalled a scene when
they were newly married, in a department store dining room,
when Atsuko had had a soda water; her straw had split and the
soda water spilled out of the tall glass. Had that been red or blue
soda water?

Atsuko had changed into her outdoor kimono without his
noticing and was sitting near his bedside.

"I told you I was going to do that," she said.

Takuji couldn't immediately recall what she meant by "that." Atsuko explained that one of her high school teachers had been awarded a medal. She was going with other senior members of the alumni association to a department store to purchase a gift for the teacher. But Takuji couldn't remember hearing this plan before.

"There's a melon cut up in the refrigerator in case you need a snack at three o'clock," she said, "but you can wait until I come home, can't you?"

Atsuko looked slim when she was dressed, but she was conscious of her plump legs and always wore a kimono for formal occasions. Takuji had long known that Atsuko had two ways of wearing a kimono, depending on whom she was seeing. When she went out with Takuji or their female relatives, she wore her kimono in the ordinary way. But when she wanted to impress other people, she pushed her bust up above the obi sash. When he had married Atsuko, her breasts were like ripe summer oranges hanging heavily on a thin tree, and he wondered how her thin frame could bear the weight. Now she was over forty, and her ripe oranges had shriveled somewhat. Judging from the way she was wearing the kimono today, Takuji suspected she was not meeting the women, as she said, but he tried not to think about it. He remembered that one feature of his illness was to be suspicious and irascible—so it said in the book he had read. According to their family doctor, Dr. Takezawa, the best medicine was to keep calm and not get upset.

Atsuko in her brand new white tabi socks quickly ran along the veranda, barely concealing her joy at going out. He called to her without realizing it.

"What is it, sir?" Atsuko turned back jokingly.

Almost crying out, Takuji suddenly knew what she reminded him of—an otter.

How many years ago was it that he had seen otters on the rooftop kiddie park of a department store? Takuji wondered. Two otters had been playing in a little pool in a corner where there was a collection of small animals for the children's amusement. He happened to be up there during his lunch break. He couldn't tell which otter was male or female, but they didn't remain still for a single moment. In great earnestness they chased dead leaves on the surface of the water as if catching fish; the next moment they floated upturned on the water with playful, carefree faces. But all the time their small, wide-set eyes seemed to be darting to and fro, always on the alert; when anyone showed the slightest sign of approaching the fish vending machine, jingling coins, they raced to the spot immediately underneath it and waited for a fish to drop when the coin was inserted, clapping their paws and uttering squeaky sounds as if begging to be fed. They were cheeky, but lovable; cunning, but friendly. That's the way they were. Fun-loving and full of life, their bodies moved almost involuntarily.

Takuji recalled another incident. Fire had broken out once in the house two doors down. Fortunately, it didn't spread. Atsuko, in her pajamas, banged an empty bucket and called out "Fire! Fire!" all over the neighborhood to wake everyone up. She seemed to enjoy herself so much that Takuji was embarrassed. Another time, when his father passed away, she had behaved in the same way; clad in a new black mourning kimono, she seemed to enjoy shedding tears. He feared that if he left her alone she would start laughing, and he nearly gave her a strong warning not to overdo the emotion.

Takuji gazed at the garden, turning over two walnut shells in his right hand. Atsuko had bought them when she learned that walnuts could be helpful in restoring the movement in his paralyzed right hand. When he turned the shells over in his good left hand, they made a lively, clicking sound, but in his right hand the sound was dull and heavy. Sitting in front of his small writing desk, Takuji tried to hold a pen, but his hand did not seem to be his own. He felt a strange combination of frustration and pain—frustration when he had pins and needles in his legs and couldn't stand up, and pain, biting pain, when he soaked himself in fresh hot water in the bathtub. When can I start writing again? he asked himself. He decided he should not think of the future, for when he did, the insects started buzzing at the base of his skull.

His garden wasn't much consolation now. He realized it had been enjoyable only when he had work to do and Atsuko stood behind him, making jokes that helped release his pent-up dissatisfaction with his job. It was similar to recess periods at school; the ball game is fun because it takes place between classes and lasts only five minutes or so. If a child is given a ball and asked to play with it the whole day long by himself, the ball becomes nothing but a rubber sphere. At times, Takuji was annoyed by Atsuko, but an otter in the house was better than nothing.

The telephone rang. He crawled to the phone to pick up the receiver. He had finally begun to pick up the telephone with his left hand and press it to his left ear. He used to listen with his right ear, but nowadays the invisible insects seemed to make noises there. The phone call was from Imazato, a close friend of Takuji since their university days. He had known him for almost forty years, and Takuji had had Atsuko contact him first before anyone else when he had fallen.

"If you have anything you want to say, tell me now. I'll be your mouthpiece," Imazato said to Takuji.

He and Takuji didn't usually exchange lengthy greetings or

remarks about the weather, but his words sounded abrupt and strange to Takuji.

"Are you really agreeing to it?" Imazato continued after a pause, "Because you used to tell me that you didn't want that at any cost. So I was wondering about it. Perhaps you can't help it, can you, because of the circumstances?"

Takuji didn't understand what he was talking about. When he then pressed Imazato to elaborate, it was the latter who became flustered.

"You really don't know about this? You truly don't know?" Imazato asked.

It had been Atsuko's idea to call a meeting, Imazato confessed, to discuss Takuji's future, and Imazato was about to attend it. Five men were to be there: Tsuboi, Takuji's superior; the owner of Makino Real Estate in the neighborhood; the deputy branch head of a nearby bank; Dr. Takezawa; and Imazato. Atsuko's plan was to demolish the house and bulldoze the garden to build an apartment block, which she planned to rent out to young bank employees and their families in return for being able to use it as collateral for a proposed bank loan. Hearing this, Takuji felt that his head was bursting. He could see Atsuko surrounded by the five men, thrusting her breasts forward, her small, shiny black eyes darting from one to the other. She would play only too well the role of a courageous and long-suffering wife. Five men. That's too many. Why Tsuboi, his superior? Takuji wondered.

Takuji didn't remember how he finished Imazato's call. Sitting and watching the garden, he recalled a painting he had seen when he was a student. Was the artist Ryuzaburo Umehara or Ryusei Kishida? Takuji, whose brain was like a cottonball, couldn't recall, but he still remembered the painting's composition. It was fairly large and depicted an old-fashioned milk bottle, flowers, a teacup, a milk jug, a half-eaten apple, a loaf of bread, and a dead pheasant, all scattered about on a table. Its title was "Otters' Festival." Takuji didn't understand the allusion to otters, and on reaching home he had checked the dictionary. Otters loved to tease. Apparently they killed numerous fish, not for eating, but just for the fun of it. They lined their captives up and gloated over them. That's why the cluttered heap was called an "otters' festival."

The fire, the funeral, her husband's illness—these were all fun to Atsuko. Takuji recalled the dead pheasant beside the milk bottle in the painting. The bird lay with its eyes opened—but their child had been dead with her eyes closed, Takuji thought.

Hoshie, their only child, had died at the age of three. The morning he was leaving on a business trip, he had touched his forehead to hers and told Atsuko that Hoshie had a fever; she should have Dr. Takezawa come and see her right away. Three days later, while he was still away on business, he received a phone call informing him that Hoshie was critically ill with pneumonia. He cut short his trip and hurried back to Tokyo, only to find a white cloth covering Hoshie's face.

Atsuko was weeping. She told him she had called Dr. Takezawa's clinic but the message had not been received correctly. Dr. Takezawa himself apologized for the delay, caused by a newly employed student nurse. Takuji's father served as a mediator between Takuji and Dr. Takezawa, settling the matter by saying, "You can't bring her back to life again even if you do sue the nurse."

He counted the age of his dead daughter every year on her birthday, but, as time passed, the memory of what had happened slowly faded away. Then one day a woman spoke to him at the station. She looked spinsterish, and he couldn't tell at first who she was. It was the nurse at Dr. Takezawa's clinic on her way back home to get married. She stood hesitantly beside him, fumbling for words, and said, "I was going to return to my old home and say nothing about it—bury the memory—but . . ." As if forcing the words out, "There was no phone call that day," she declared. She told him it was the following day that Atsuko had phoned Dr. Takezawa, asking him to come and see Hoshie. On the day Takuji left for his business trip, Atsuko had had a class reunion.

That night Takuji got drunk. Very drunk. When he returned home, he wanted to slap Atsuko across the face as soon as she opened the front door. But he didn't.

Why? Why didn't he do it? Takuji tried to remember the reason, but the insects started buzzing again. He must have thought he shouldn't raise his hand to this woman. He had simply walked quietly into the house and fallen asleep, numbed by the alcohol.

The thin gray dawn light filtered through the garden. Takuji couldn't have cared less about the pine trees, the maple trees, and the stone carving with five ringlets. His head felt at its worst at this time of day. He had no interest in the garden now. Before long everything would be gone, replaced by a cheap brick building.

He heard Atsuko's voice. She was talking to their neighbor's wife, who had asked after Takuji. In her sing-song voice, as if she were talking about the next day's weather, Atsuko was telling the neighbor about his blood pressure.

Takuji got up. Hanging onto the frames of the paper screen doors, he went to the kitchen. Before he realized it, he was clutching a big knife. He wasn't sure whether to plunge it into his own chest or Atsuko's ample bosom.

"Hey! That's great!" It was Atsuko. "You *have* improved—now you can hold a knife. It's only a matter of time before you're completely well," she said in a happy voice. Her small dark eyes, like watermelon seeds, set far apart, were shining and animated.

"I just wanted some melon," Takuji said. Dropping the knife in the sink, he walked back toward the veranda facing the garden. The insects had started making their noises at the back of his head.

"Speaking of melons, which would you prefer? The one from the bank or the real estate agent's?" Atsuko asked.

Takuji couldn't answer her. As if a camera clicked closed, the garden suddenly went black.

Manhattan

SINCE HIS WIFE LEFT HIM, MUTSUO HAD LEARNED MANY things. Bread, for instance, went stale in three days, and got moldy within a week. A French baguette became a club after a month. A bottle of milk went sour after a week—even in the refrigerator. Ah, refrigerators. One day Mutsuo had found a plastic bag of green water at the bottom of his. He couldn't recall buying any green ice cream. After wondering exactly what it was, he realized it was the bag of cucumbers his wife, Sugiko, had bought before she left him three months before. In junior high school he had learned that cucumbers consisted of ninety-seven or ninety-eight percent water. Well, that's certainly true, Mutsuo thought, finally understanding what he had been taught in his youth. Ever since, he had been reluctant to open the refrigerator.

Slumped on the living room sofa, Mutsuo would fall asleep, watching late night movies, and be awakened at dawn by the noise of the television. When he slept in the double bed, he found that his arms and body would move as if to embrace another body next to him. So he had gotten into the habit of sleeping on the sofa even though the unnatural postures he assumed there inevitably produced painful joints by morning. As he stretched and rubbed his limbs to ease the ache, he would hear the rustle of the morning paper being pushed into his mailbox on the front door. He would smoke a cigarette as he read the paper from cover to cover, from the advertisements for condominiums, which he had no intention of buying, to the five steps for catching flounder in the fishing section. But Mutsuo would never look at the help wanted pages.

After reading the paper, he would lie back on the sofa again and doze off. At eleven o'clock he would get up and wash his face, and look at himself in the mirror splattered with white toothpaste. He saw the bloated features of a jobless, thirty-eight-year-old man. The air was stale, and time stood still.

At eleven-thirty, Mutsuo would put on a pair of sandals and go to a nearby Chinese restaurant, the Yoraiken, where he would order a plate of crispy noodles. The noodles weren't easy to eat because the tips of them always stuck to the plate, but he wanted to make things difficult for himself. Sometimes he thought about ordering other dishes, but, when seated, he always found himself asking for the usual plate of crispy noodles.

Mutsuo had been following the same routine for three months now. The only challenge he had was the noodles at the Yoraiken. Only when he ate them did he feel alive; the rest of the time he was like a dead man. With the rental income from an apartment, his late mother's legacy, he wasn't short of money, but he thought he should find a job while he was still getting unemployment benefits. Yet he knew very well that he could not find a better job than he had had before. A salaried clerk had virtually no marketable skills.

After lunch, his toothpick in his mouth, he would drop in at the bookshop, buy a weekly magazine, and meander home. On his way back, he would catch sight of his own figure in a shop window. He looked exactly like the long French baguette in the kitchen. "You're so apathetic," Sugiko used to scold.

Suddenly pain shot to the top of his head—his toothpick

must have touched the nerve in his bad tooth. I should've had my teeth fixed before she left me. The idea suddenly crossed his mind, but he quickly dismissed it with a wry smile. That's a bit stingy; no wonder my wife left me, he thought.

Sugiko was a dentist. She was beautiful, with a practical mind. If they had had sushi delivered to the house to feed their guests, she would pick off and eat all the sliced fish from the tops of any leftover pieces. Sushi was expensive, she said, and fish was nutritious, and it would be a waste of money to return the leftovers as they were, with the fish still on top of the rice. She was probably right, but seven or eight small loaves of rice scattered on a black lacquered tray minus the fish appeared somewhat mean to Mutsuo. On these occasions, Sugiko's sculpted face, which Mutsuo had adored when he was in love with her, looked vulgar.

Sugiko had her way in everything and loved to force her views onto others. When Mutsuo tried to have black coffee, she said it would be bad for his stomach and added a teaspoonful of sugar.

Perhaps because of this tendency of hers Mutsuo had dreamed, at dawn, that he was walking along a corridor. He seemed to be in a building or an apartment. When he knocked on the door and opened it, Mutsuo saw himself seated in the center of a large, empty room having his teeth worked on by Sugiko. Below the neck he was covered by a white gown so that he looked like a white tent. The moment he noticed his other self in the chair, he was swiftly transformed into that other self. He couldn't remember what to call the drill that dug out teeth cavities with such a horrible noise, but white granulated sugar was pouring out of the end of its shaft. Mutsuo's mouth was full of the sugar; it overflowed, forming a large pyramid on the floor. Painful. Sweet. Dull. He was tired of holding his mouth open.

Mutsuo, without realizing it, had switched places with the other Mutsuo, who was now watching him from the corridor. And it was not Sugiko who was treating him; it was Inada, a dentist who had recruited Sugiko the year before to come work at the modern dental clinic he ran. Mutsuo had met him only once, but he vividly recalled the gold ring he wore on his little finger, and his broad neck and shoulders, hinting at a suppressed vitality. Sugiko had been exceptionally polite to Inada when she introduced Mutsuo to him. Later, Mutsuo realized their affair had already begun.

Granulated sugar still spilled noisily from his mouth, forming a shiny white pile on his chest and in front of him. "Oh, it hurts! It's hurting me!" Mutsuo cried out, waking.

The television was making the same hiss as the sugar. White stripes flickered on the screen because the station had gone off the air.

Mutsuo would walk along the very edge of the road, so close to the mortar fence that his shoulder almost touched it. It wasn't that an unemployed man shouldn't walk in the center of the road; he just wanted to walk along the edge. Once he had decided on a course of action, as with the crispy Chinese noodles, he would feel restless until he had seen it through. And then he would repeat what he had done. After the Chinese restaurant, he would go to the bookshop, buy his magazine, and return to his apartment by the same route. Arriving home, he would go straight to the kitchen, touch the French baguette leaning against the wall to check its hardness, and drink a glass of water. Then he would lie down on the sofa, read the periodical from cover to cover, start drinking beer when the seven o'clock news came on, and call out for dinner. This was his daily routine.

But this day, things didn't go as usual. The road he usually took was blocked by a truck. One of the shops by the road was being demolished, and workmen were carrying old timbers away from the site. He was in an alley running behind the main road, and since it was blocked by the truck and clouds of dust were rising in the air, Mutsuo knew he should make a detour and return to the main road. But he didn't. He was determined to follow his route. If he changed to another one, his whole routine would collapse.

His eyes half-closed to avoid the dust, Mutsuo realized that the shop being demolished was the one that until yesterday had sold croquettes. It was run by an elderly couple, and after his wife left him Mutsuo had occasionally stopped in. There had been no sign that it was to be torn down. Demolitions and remodeling were rather like a cuckolded husband: before one realized it, the affair was far advanced.

"What's going on? Is a new shop being built?" Mutsuo asked the foreman.

Without speaking, the foreman tapped the board that displayed the construction permit. The name of the new shop was to be Manhattan.

A few days later, Mutsuo met Sugiko to discuss their pending divorce in a coffee shop.

"Listen. Do listen to me," Sugiko said to Mutsuo. Sugiko's lipstick had become darker since their separation. Sitting across the table, she looked five or six years younger than she really was. She spoke harshly, but her gestures were feminine. The manner she reserved for her new man inadvertently slipped out, revealing itself to the man she was divorcing. Mutsuo listened to her talk: "It wasn't that I disliked you because you became withdrawn. It was the way you responded to your life—not trying very hard to find a new job—that made me feel dissatisfied with my life. I thought we would get along better when your mother died. But no, our personalities clashed, didn't they? I'm glad we didn't have any children."

Mutsuo heard all of what Sugiko said, but he thought he could also hear other voices somewhere. "Manhattan. Manhattan," they said, like an endlessly looping tape.

When it was finished, Manhattan, he discovered, would be a tiny bar and cocktail lounge of the sort that would hold only a dozen or so patrons. Mutsuo felt compelled to go see how the construction was progressing several times a day—when he got up, during the afternoon, and in the evening. Because of its shoddy construction, the shop would change greatly in appearance if he didn't see it for even half a day. Why am I so concerned with this? Mutsuo asked himself. Is there something about the name, Manhattan? he wondered. But no matter how hard he tried, he couldn't find any reason for his obsession.

"Manhattan. Manhattan." The word went round and round in Mutsuo's mind, all day long, like a tiny mouse on an exercise wheel. Was it that he liked the sound of the word or did he simply need something to make a sound inside his head? As long as the wheel turned he didn't have to think about his unemployment, Sugiko calling him "apathetic," or the piercing, curious eyes of the other apartment residents as they looked at the husband whose wife had fled. He still went to the Yoraiken for lunch, but he began to order cold noodles instead of the warm crispy noodle plate. He also started to change from his day clothes into pajamas. Sometimes he slept on the bed instead of the sofa. At dawn he might find his arm stretched out next to him, but he felt he was embracing Manhattan instead of his wife.

Sugiko stood up, saying she would contact him again to sign the divorce papers and collect her belongings.

"Your job—you haven't found one yet?" Sugiko asked as she reached for the bill.

Mutsuo didn't flinch. A thousand yen or so, whoever paid, it didn't matter. Two days later Manhattan would be open anyway.

On his way back from the coffee shop to his apartment, Mutsuo dropped by the construction site. Now they were working on the interior. The workmen Mutsuo had gotten to know said they would work all night to meet the deadline for the opening day.

"Shall I bring you some food? It must be tiring," Mutsuo offered.

"Thanks, but no thank you. That would be imposing. The mama-san will bring something to eat, I bet," an older man said, as he pasted up wallpaper.

"Is that so? I see. Manhattan has a mama-san," Mutsuo said. He almost asked the man if she was beautiful, but told himself not to rush. He could find out on opening day.

As Mutsuo was about to leave the site, something hit him, knocking him to the ground. One of the workers, who was trying to attach the signboard, had dropped a small tool. Had it landed directly on Mutsuo, it could have produced a serious injury, but fortunately it just grazed the edge of his head. Still, blood streamed out between his fingers as he pressed them against the wound. He was taken to a nearby hospital for a brain scan and was kept there overnight just to make sure it was nothing serious.

The construction manager soon came to see him in the hospital. Although he apologized, he made it clear that Mutsuo's presence on the construction site had been unauthorized, and the accident had occurred just as he was leaving it. Perhaps the company was taking precautions lest Mutsuo sue them for the accident. Mutsuo had no intention of doing that, and frankly didn't care who was responsible; he just wanted the man to go away and leave him alone as soon as possible. He was in fact sorry that his wound wasn't more serious. He wished a hammer had dropped on his head and killed him. Then he could have had a love-suicide with Manhattan. Before too long the mama-san would come. The mama-san of Manhattan would pay a visit to the hospital, he thought to himself. By sheer accident Mutsuo was going to have a closer relationship with Manhattan and the mama-san than any future customers. The mouse in Mutsuo's head spun the wheel louder and more frenziedly: "Manhattan. Manhattan."

Contrary to Mutsuo's expectations, the mama-san wasn't a striking beauty. She was thin and looked rather like a short version of Olive Oyl, Popeye's girlfriend. She was about thirty years old with a dark complexion. She placed a basket of fruit she must have bought at an all-night supermarket on the table beside his bed. It was one of those get-well baskets that looked nice but had a raised bottom so it held less fruit. When a child of the patient sharing his room came near them, the mama-san smiled and said, "Is this yours?"

"I don't have a wife. It would be terrible if I had a child," Mutsuo said.

The mama-san looked surprised.

Mutsuo suddenly recalled a conversation he had had with his boss when he was in the commercial section. "So, what do you think of our opening day?" his boss had asked him.

"Well, I think sales went very well," Mutsuo had answered. "Manhattan. Manhattan." Things were going as well as could be expected. That night Mutsuo slept soundly for the first time in three months.

On Manhattan's opening night, Mutsuo received the most attention of all the customers there. The white bandage on his head spoke most eloquently of who he was. He felt the place belonged to him. Newly opened shops often lack many things, and when he heard Manhattan had run out of lemons, he woke up a fruit shop owner and persuaded him to wrap up all the lemons in the shop for him.

Mutsuo visited Manhattan every night. After five days, his bandage was removed. He missed it, but its effect lingered, and he remained a special customer. Mutsuo reciprocated as much as possible. When he heard Hatta, another regular customer, tell the mama-san, "This chair looks nice, but it hurts my butt," and the mama-san apologizing, he dashed to his apartment to bring back a suitable cushion for the chair and donated it to the shop.

"I was wondering why this place looked bare. Now I know why. One of the walls has no decoration," Hatta said. He was quite observant.

"Sorry. Paintings are so expensive," the mama-san replied.

Mutsuo ran back to his apartment again to fetch a lithograph from the living room. Returning to Manhattan, he began to put it on the wall without a word. After hammering in the nails and raising the lithograph on the right side according to Hatta's direction, he adjusted the cord. At this moment the mama-san leaned on his back.

Well, Olive isn't that bad after all, Mutsuo thought to himself. He liked her. She was the same type of person he was. This woman would not eat the fish off of leftover sushi.

In the early evening, before sunset, Mutsuo would leave his apartment and visit Manhattan. He didn't proceed along the edge of the road any more, followed by his long, slightly stooping shadow. Mutsuo, the French baguette, and the mama-san, Olive, seemed to be a good combination, he mused.

After a month or so, Mutsuo began to tell the mama-san about himself when there weren't many customers around. He told her how his dentist wife had taken a lover and left him; how his company had gone bankrupt and he was jobless, but thanks to the rent from an apartment his mother had left him he wasn't in a particular hurry to find a job—he confided everything to her. He tried to persuade her to come to his apartment, only two streets away, to listen to his records, and he waited until closing time. But Hatta, the other regular, also stayed on. So Mutsuo went back to his apartment alone.

Soon, he heard someone tapping on the door. It was a careful knock, one not wishing to wake the neighbors. Mutsuo was undressing to take a bath. He called out, quickly put on his trousers, kicked the hard French baguette into a closet, and opened the door, expecting to see the mama-san. But no one was there. It looked as if she had decided against it at the last moment.

Oh, well. It's come this far, so it's simply a matter of time, he thought to himself. We two apathetic people, let's take it slowly, shall we?

"Manhattan. Manhattan." The great chorus of rejoicing made by the mouse could be quite deafening, but nowadays it had toned down somewhat, perhaps because he was content.

Mutsuo had an argument with Sugiko when she came to remove her belongings still left in the apartment.

"Where's my lithograph?" she asked.

They had lived together for nearly ten years, so it was hard knowing what belonged to whom. It would be easy to get the drawing back from Manhattan, but that would, he feared, cut off what he had nurtured and what had begun to bear fruit. So Mutsuo offered to repay Sugiko.

Sugiko stared at him. "Where did you take it?" she asked.

He recalled the same accusing eyes, the eyes his mother had directed at his father, who had left home because of a young woman twenty years ago. His father often took many things out of the house: scrolls of brush pictures, Noh masks, a new radio. Judging from Sugiko's jealous face, Mutsuo suspected she wasn't getting along very well with her man. If only Mutsuo could say, "I'll seriously look for a job. Promise. Shall we try all over again?" he felt that the two of them could get back together again. But he pressed his seal on the divorce papers in silence.

"Manhattan. Manhattan." The mouse was turning the wheel slowly.

A month passed without any concrete progress on either the job hunt or the romance with the mama-san. It was raining on Monday, but to make up for Sunday, when Manhattan did not open, he left his apartment earlier than usual, only to find that the bar was closed. In front of it were a liquor store owner and a butcher loudly demanding money for unpaid bills from the landlord. Apparently he and the mama-san had had a disagreement about the lease, and she had bolted without settling up. Now Mutsuo realized for the first time that Hatta was the mama-san's husband and that the name of the bar, Manhattan, was taken from his surname.

"Manhattan. Manhattan." The mouse turning the wheel died.

When Mutsuo returned to his apartment, sinking down on the sofa, his decayed tooth began to ache. There was a knocking at the door. Very hesitant knocking. Yes, it was the mama-san's knocking. She had come to return the lithograph. When he opened the door, a stranger, an old man, was standing there.

"Do you have any umbrellas you want repaired?" the old man asked, visibly agitated.

"No," Mutsuo said, closing the door.

It occurred to him that he had never heard of an umbrella repairman calling on customers at night. He could be a very clever thief, he imagined. Suddenly a realization flashed through his mind. He had seen the old man's face somewhere. Like the French baguette in the kitchen, leaning against the kitchen wall, it was brown, dry, and hard. Could it be his father who had left home twenty years ago?

He heard the now familiar knock again. It was hesitant, as if not wishing the neighbors to know. Could that knock have been his instead of the mama-san's that other night? I thought it was hers. Is he here because the woman left him, or is he short of money? Once I open the door he'll sit on the sofa, watch television the whole day long, and eat crispy Chinese noodles.

His late mother had always said to Mutsuo, "You're exactly like your father."

The knocking continued.

Beef Shoulder

THE ODOR OF MOTHBALLS SEEMED TO PENETRATE HIS WHOLE body, Hanzawa felt, following him everywhere he went in the house. The source of the smell was his wife's kimono. Miki-ko had taken it out of storage in the kimono chest and hung it up to air. They were invited to a wedding that evening. The bride, Hatsuko Omachi, had been Hanzawa's secretary for five years.

Mikiko was always overdoing things. She liked heavy doses of salt and pepper on her food, for example. Hanzawa wanted to tell her she had used too many mothballs, but he refrained. It was better for him not to say anything unnecessary until the reception was over, he thought.

Hanzawa looked carefully at himself in the bathroom mirror. He was not yet fifty, but his beard was already sprinkled with white hairs. His wife had had white hairs first. The year before last she had started dyeing her hair. At first, she had hidden the dye at the very back of the shelf in the closet so Hanzawa wouldn't find it. Nowadays she had become careless, leaving the dye by the wash basin. Perhaps it was yesterday she had dyed her hair, but it seemed she had taken particular pains over it this time.

The problem will be when I walk into the reception room, thought Hanzawa, pressing his left cheek. When I go in and greet the bride at the entrance, this must not twitch.

Whenever he tried to hide an inner agitation, his left cheek betrayed him by twitching. His wife couldn't help but notice. Hanzawa forced himself to think of Hatsuko's bony shoulders in her navy blue uniform as she sat and typed letters, and of her modest manner as she gave them to him for his signature. He reminded himself, too, about how she used to come to his house with her colleagues on New Year's Day and play a picture-card game with his children.

But he shouldn't think about those other days.

About this time last year, it had become apparent that Hatsuko was making mistakes in her work. She wasn't particularly skilled, but she had done accurate work. When messages began to be left unconveyed and typing errors uncorrected, Hanzawa could no longer ignore the matter. He had heard rumors that her fiance had left her. So after work, he invited her for dinner and asked if she would care to discuss her problem. Hatsuko confided that she had a bedridden father nearing retirement age and that her fiance had jilted her at the very last minute. But she quickly added, "That doesn't matter anymore; it's all over now." Then she smiled, and replied, "Rare, please," to the waiter asking how she wanted her steak cooked.

"It's rare isn't it, when it's undercooked?" she asked.

"That's right. You should eat it with the blood still coming out. That'll give you energy, and tomorrow you'll feel like a new woman."

Hatsuko nodded as he spoke, then said seriously, "Mr. Hanzawa, could I ask you a favor?"

"What is it?" he asked.

"Would you take me to an amusement park, please?"

Another executive of the company had once described Hatsuko as "a girl with the face of a cheap *hina* doll." The *hina* dolls that Hanzawa's family displayed for their annual celebration of Girl's Day in March had been brought by his late mother from her home when she married. The dolls were old and finely made, so Hanzawa had never really looked at the cheap, modern *hina* dolls. After hearing his colleague's comments, Hanzawa studied Hatsuko carefully; she did indeed have the eyes, nose, and mouth of a passable beauty, but she lacked the quality of a well-made *hina* doll. Her velvety skin was her most outstanding feature, and she had a doll's figure—thin and not at its best in Western clothes. When she looked directly into his eyes in the subdued light of the restaurant, Hanzawa sensed an unexpected force, and he couldn't deny her request.

That night at the amusement park, Hatsuko fired the gun like a madwoman. When a hundred-yen coin was inserted, UFOs appeared one after another on the screen, and she shot at them. She said she wouldn't go home until she had racked up three hundred points. She left her handbag with Hanzawa. "Damn you! Fuck you!" tumbled from her mouth as she fired. Large tears rolled down her cheeks.

Hanzawa couldn't let her go home in that condition. He took her to a bar nearby, where they had drinks, and—the rest—he couldn't describe it other than to say he was simply overcome by a demon.

He returned home after midnight. Mikiko opened the door, shocking him with her face, which had turned reddish purple and was so swollen that her eyes and lips were almost closed. A new dye was responsible, she said. Hanzawa blamed himself. He had had several affairs in the past, but never one with his secretary. I'll say that the drinking made me do it, he thought to himself.

From that day, Hanzawa adopted an inscrutable countenance and tried to avoid Hatsuko's eyes. About a week later, she came to get his signature. "Da-da-da-da," she murmured, like the sound of a gun firing, before walking back to her desk. Hatsuko was only five years older than his eldest daughter, Hanzawa realized. He thought of his wife's swollen, discolored face, yet he found himself walking again to the shooting gallery in the amusement park.

Hatsuko was shooting UFOs at the same machine as before. She wasn't crying, but watching her press the large gun to her frail shoulder, Hanzawa couldn't ignore her. He put his hand on her shoulder. They went to the same bar and the same hotel, the same as before, but this time his body didn't perform. As he lay on the bed in embarrassment, Hatsuko silently guided his hand under the sheet, and pressed it to her abdomen. There he felt a small bump the size of a tangerine seed in the area of her large intestine. She told him how she had gotten it.

In the spring of her second year in junior high school, crocheting was in vogue, but it was prohibited at school because some students in the back of the classroom would keep crocheting, even during class. Hatsuko was one of many who ignored the ban. One day, neglecting the room-cleaning chores the students had all been assigned, Hatsuko was working away at her crocheting when she was almost caught by her old spinster teacher. In a panic, Hatsuko thrust the hook and cotton thread into her school uniform's skirt pocket and bent down to mop the floor. This pushed the tip of the hook into her abdomen. She was immediately taken to the school doctor, but due either to bad doctoring or the way her body reacted, the scar remained.

"You know the sound when you make a hole with a toothpick in a ground cherry? It was like that when the hook went into my belly," Hatsuko said.

She is telling me this embarrassing experience of hers to

make me feel better, Hanzawa thought. He was surprised; he felt ten years younger.

Again he went home after midnight. His wife opened the door, the swelling on her face half gone. He knew that his left cheek was twitching as he looked at her. Oh, no. This is too dangerous. If I keep seeing Hatsuko, the tic will get much worse, he thought.

Hanzawa suggested to his superior that Hatsuko be transferred out of his section, and before long she had moved to a different building. He had hardly seen her since, and she didn't come to his house on New Year's Day as she had for the past five years.

"I wonder why Miss Omachi didn't come this year?" Mikiko said, glancing at him as she wrapped up the lacquerware sake cups that had been used for the holidays.

"Perhaps she went to the new boss's place. People are like that," Hanzawa said. He meant to smile at her, but he felt his left cheek start to twitch.

In March the *hina* dolls were decorated for Girl's Day. On his way back from the bathroom in the middle of night, walking to his bedroom through the living room, where the dolls were being displayed, he stopped and looked at them in the dark. Their faces were like Hatsuko's on that night, in his arms with her eyes closed. There were three "lady-in-waiting" dolls, and the one on the right in particular resembled Hatsuko. He felt a sudden urge to take off the doll's skirt. Act your age, he laughed to himself, and returned to bed. He missed the tiny tangerine seed on Hatsuko's belly that his fingers remembered so well, and he felt a sudden revulsion at his wife's heavy features as she slept next to him.

When Hanzawa unexpectedly received an invitation

addressed to "Mr. and Mrs. Hanzawa" to attend Hatsuko's wedding and reception, he felt his left cheek begin to twitch again. Hatsuko's invitation to both of them was not in itself unusual, for she had been to his house in the past, and Hanzawa's wife had once sent her a silk scarf or some other little gift. But she had been transferred out of his department. Getting the wedding invitation was like being stuck by a safety pin.

"I don't think you need to go," Hanzawa said to his wife, trying to sound casual. He was about to put only his name on the reply card. But Mikiko insisted on going. She wanted an opportunity to wear the kimono she had purchased at the end of the previous year. And she suggested they give 20,000 yen, twice as much as they normally would for a wedding. "She was very good to you," Mikiko explained. All this made Hanzawa heavy-hearted.

At the wedding, Hanzawa's worries proved groundless. Just before he entered the reception hall, he was delayed by a former female employee and was thus not accompanied by his wife. The go-between couple, the bride and the bridegroom, and their parents all stood in the entrance hall to receive the guests. Small queues of people waited their turn to congratulate the couple. Hatsuko looked surprisingly gorgeous, like a different woman, perhaps because of her heavy make-up. The small middle-aged woman in a kimono beside her, resembling an old *hina* doll, must have been Hatsuko's mother. Hanzawa hated walking past her; it was rather like going through the X-ray gate at the airport prior to boarding a plane.

"Congratulations! Many congratulations!" Hanzawa greeted Hatsuko in a voice he knew was much too loud. But when he spoke in a loud voice, smiling, his left cheek behaved itself.

Hatsuko accepted his greeting, pleasantly introducing him as "my former superior" to the tall bridegroom as she glanced up at him. He seemed good-natured enough. In his rented white tuxedo, he looked just like a singer making his debut.

After all the guests were seated, the bride and bridegroom entered the reception hall. During the applause, Mikiko leaned toward Hanzawa. "I think Miss Omachi's pregnant. Haven't you noticed?" she whispered.

Hanzawa caught the whiff of strong perfume around Mikiko's ear. He hadn't noticed it in the taxi on their way to the reception; she must have put it on after they arrived. She had a habit of tipping the small bottle of perfume on the end of her little finger and then dabbing herself.

"Perhaps three months, possibly four months pregnant," Mikiko continued.

Hanzawa didn't want to reply. That thin belly like an empty purse would swell up into a white balloon. Then what would happen to the little tangerine seed there? Was the bridegroom, sweating in his white tuxedo, allowed to touch it? Hanzawa suspected that he wasn't. He remembered the face of the *hina* doll he had seen in the dark in his living room. As he listened to the wedding march, he noticed he was caressing the back of his left hand with his middle right finger. Mikiko was clapping her hands, leaning forward on the table. She hasn't suspected us yet. I thought she had. Perhaps I was too anxious, he thought. Hanzawa, too, clapped heartily.

On their way home in the taxi Hanzawa dozed off. Intoxication had come quicker than usual because he had used up so much nervous energy earlier in the day. Besides, not wanting to start a conversation with Mikiko in the taxi, he had pretended to be asleep and then actually fell asleep. What a rotten person I am, Hanzawa was thinking.

Shaking Hanzawa awake to tell him they were almost home, Mikiko said, giving a small laugh, "The bride's probably taking a catnap in the bullet train by now." Hanzawa felt a slight twinge, but that was all; his left cheek remained still. On such a night, he thought, the best thing was to take a hot bath, watch silly programs on the television, have a nightcap, and go to bed early.

When he opened the front door, however, an unexpected face greeted him. It was Tamon, his friend from university days. Hanzawa and Tamon had been close, and they had visited each other every day while at school together, but for a time they had drifted apart. About ten years ago, after running into each other in the corridor of a Japanese restaurant they both used for company entertaining, they had resumed their friendship. Now they saw each other once every six months or so. Yet this was the first time Tamon had waited for him like this.

"No, there's no special reason for coming to see you," Tamon said. By chance, he had been near Hanzawa's house, and when he phoned, he was told they were out at a wedding. Thinking they would return shortly, Tamon had invited himself in and helped himself to a whiskey. He gestured to Hanzawa with his hand as if holding a tumbler and drinking the contents.

Hanzawa worried that Tamon had lost weight in the last half year. "Unlike your well-established company, mine's sandwiched between the unions and the poor economy. I have no time to put on weight," Tamon said, laughing off Hanzawa's concern. But he had deep, dark circles under his eyes.

Soon the drinking began. Since both of them had already been drinking, they became drunk in less than half the time it would have taken in a bar. Mikiko, who didn't drink, had some sweet wine and waited on them, sitting between the two.

"Is there anything I'm supposed to return to you? Anything at all?" Tamon suddenly asked. Hanzawa had no recollection that Tamon owed him anything. When they were younger, they used to borrow and lend. For a time Hanzawa's wallet was also Tamon's, and they shared one dictionary between the two of them. But now, their friendship wasn't that close. When Hanzawa pointed this out, Tamon nodded in agreement and said, "I once had a narrow escape from death, thanks to you. I came to the end of the line and was contemplating suicide. I was fed up with everything then and couldn't have cared less." Hanzawa could roughly guess when that was.

Twenty-five years ago Tamon had got tuberculosis soon after he graduated from school and got a job with a fairly good company. He had taken a nonsalaried leave for one year and checked himself into a sanatorium in a suburb of Tokyo. Around that time, a new medicine, streptomycin, had just arrived on the market, and tuberculosis was no longer a fatal illness. Still, dropping out of the company rat race for nearly a year was the same as deserting the front lines while the war was on.

Hanzawa was unhappy at about the same time. His mother had adamantly refused to accept his marriage proposal to Mikiko, who had been his girlfriend since his university days. His mother disapproved of Mikiko because she had briefly worked part-time at a bar in Shinjuku in order to help pay her school expenses. "Spare me from anyone who would crook her little finger and hold a cup of tea!" Hanzawa's mother would say. During the time immediately after the war, when the yen was switched from old to new valuations and everyone was having financial difficulties, she had taken a side job at home making overcoats out of army blankets to help her son get through school. Hanzawa didn't have the nerve to leave home against her will.

Because of these obstacles, Hanzawa gradually fell out of the habit of visiting Tamon with Mikiko every two weeks. When both of them did call on Tamon, he would be concerned about their marriage, almost as if it were his own, and accuse Hanzawa of being a coward. With nothing better to do in his sick bed, Hanzawa's romance seemed to be the only thing that kept Tamon going. Hanzawa grew tired of making excuses for not having married Mikiko yet. Mikiko, however, apparently had visited Tamon, who was her only ally, even after Hanzawa had stopped going to see him. After a few ups and downs, Hanzawa married Mikiko about a year later. Tamon eventually left the sanatorium, idled away three months in his apartment, and then got the job at his current company. Hanzawa guessed that it was at about this time that Tamon's situation became extreme.

A large bottle of spirits. Three rolls of tape for sealing the windows. Socks with holes and soiled underwear stuffed in a *furoshiki* wrapping cloth, thrown into the Shibuya River on his way to a bathhouse. All he had to do was go home to his apartment, close up the windows as he drank the liquor, and turn on the gas. That would certainly free him from his problems. Then a book he had borrowed from Hanzawa suddenly popped into his mind.

"I remembered that on the back cover you had written, 'Please return. Don't forget,' and I had gone and lent it to someone else. So I went to Daikanyama to get the book back from my friend, and then came to your house to return it," Tamon told them.

Hanzawa's house was in the Sangenjaya area near Shibuya, which was not so far away. Tamon walked along a dark, narrow road, carrying the book. There were few lighted streets in Tokyo then, and there were still patches of land filled with war debris. Tamon heard the cries of babies coming from low-roofed houses that had escaped the bombs and fires. From a drain came the smell and steam of hot water probably used for bathing.

"That smell. It defeated me. It certainly did. After that, I felt killing myself was just stupid," Tamon said quietly to himself, filling Hanzawa's whiskey glass, which held only melted ice.

Mikiko let out a big sigh as if she had been holding her breath, stood up, and opened a window, the same window Tamon had knocked on from outside that day, pressing the book on Hanzawa in silence when it opened. Then Tamon had turned his back and walked away. Hanzawa recalled this incident vaguely. He had been preoccupied with getting the money he needed for the wedding, too preoccupied to look closely at the eyes of the friend who had come to return his book.

"You don't remember the title of the book, do you? It was *My Observation of the West* by Toyoichiro Nogami. It had a charcoal sketch of a bullfight by Goya," said Tamon.

Hanzawa didn't recall this either.

After Mikiko got up to prepare supper in the kitchen, Tamon stopped talking and gazed through the window at the garden.

Mikiko had been slender back then. Men and women all over Japan had no meat on their bones, but Mikiko was particularly thin. She often wore a white sharkskin suit, a fashionable choice at the time, and she continued to wear it even after the collar became soiled. Hanzawa didn't know whether she wanted to be seen in her best suit or whether she simply didn't have many other clothes to wear. On one occasion he found a small green spot on her skirt. "Oh, I got that sitting on the grass while I was talking to a friend of mine," Mikiko said. Hanzawa wondered if merely sitting on the grass would make such a green spot. When he turned his eyes to her handbag, he noticed that its handle had apparently been torn off and then clumsily stitched to the cowhide. "A German shepherd at a friend's house pulled it off while he was playing," Mikiko had explained with a smile. Was the dog Tamon? Hanzawa had wondered then, for he had heard a rumor that a patient had sneaked out of the sanatorium for a rendezvous in the grove behind the buildings. Hanzawa recalled that it was immediately after this that Tamon had come to return his book.

Mikiko reentered the room carrying a steaming pot with large pieces of beef and white radishes. "I sent my son to the butcher, and he bought this shoulder meat by mistake. Perhaps you won't like it," Mikiko apologized.

It was an inexpensive cut of beef, but having cooked for hours it was tender and tasty. Both Tamon and Mikiko took large pieces of meat and began to chew. Mikiko's lips, a darker shade than usual, shone with the fat from the meat as if they were a separate living creature. They pulled in the beef and sent it back and down the throat. Tamon, who to Hanzawa seemed not quite as animated as usual, ate well. The inside of his mouth, perhaps due to the light, looked like fresh red meat.

"Cattle are strange, aren't they?" Tamon said. "They only eat grass, so how do they turn out such meat and fat?"

"Speaking of fat," Mikiko joined in, wiping the grease from her lips, "beef has more fat than pork, I think."

All three agreed that beef was tastier than pork; they kept eating the beef.

Everyday life, daily life, continues uneventfully. Munching grass in silence eventually turns it to meat and fat, Hanzawa thought. Hatsuko, with her thin shoulders, chest, and hips, would grow to be like Mikiko in twenty years. As Mikiko had discreetly kept her own counsel, so, too, would Hatsuko, becoming a plump, mature woman.

"I'm going away next week," Tamon said. He was being admitted to a clinic for a work-up on his stomach and intestines.

"Are you all right, eating this fatty beef?" Mikiko asked.

Not replying, Tamon stretched his chopsticks to the meat in the pot.

Twenty-five years ago Tamon had saved his own life by coming to Hanzawa to return his book. What did he come to return tonight? Hanzawa wondered. Was Tamon just being superstitious?

Hanzawa also took a big chunk of meat.

The Doghouse

TATSUKO HAD BECOME QUITE ADEPT AT PREDICTING WHICH passengers would get off at the next station—perhaps because she tired so easily now. In three months, her swollen middle would probably guarantee her a seat on a train without asking. Now was perhaps the worst time because it wasn't so conspicuous yet. When the loudspeaker began to announce the next stop, Tatsuko, who was holding onto a strap, would look around at the eyes of the seated passengers. Their faces were expressionless, but Tatsuko could detect the ones who would soon be getting off—they became restless, or their eyes darted here and there. If Tatsuko quickly went to stand in front of one of them, she could always get a seat.

The train was crowded this late Sunday afternoon. At the station, Tatsuko grabbed a seat using her usual ploy, but this was a major junction anyway; many families on their way home had gotten off, and a cool breeze began to circulate through the train.

A couple and their child, a boy about five years old, were sitting opposite Tatsuko. All three, with the boy in the middle, were asleep; their necks slumped forward as if broken. They did not look well-off, but probably in response to the boy's nagging they had dressed up and gone to the zoo or somewhere and now were on their way home. The only thing that seemed out of character was the large, expensive-looking camera the man's hands were holding tightly against his chest. Those hands were the hands of a laborer, not of a man who pushed a pen to make his living. His wife, in her late twenties, around Tatsuko's age, was sound asleep with her knees wide open, her legs forming the sides of a rhombus. A plump and carefree type of woman. Then Tatsuko realized she was pregnant. Since becoming pregnant herself, Tatsuko had had to learn to predict which passengers were getting off, but she seemed to *sense* when a woman was pregnant. They're just like our family, she thought. Perhaps she'll deliver a month or two before I do, but her husband's and son's ages are the same as mine.

The only difference was that her husband was asleep at home. An anesthetist at a university hospital, he slept in on Sundays when he had had several operations the preceding week. It was as if he himself was anesthetized—from consuming so much nervous energy. Because of his habit of sleeping in on weekends, their son, who had turned five, had not yet seen the panda at the zoo. Tatsuko watched the couple and their son through the legs of the swaying straphangers in front of her. Which family is happier? Them or us? she wondered.

The train suddenly lurched to a halt just after leaving a station; possibly a signal had changed. The husband sitting opposite Tatsuko woke up, raised his head in surprise, and cast his eyes outside the train, thinking that they had missed their destination. Tatsuko stifled a gasp of surprise when she saw the man's face. It was Katchan, Katchan from the Uotomi Fish Shop. Tatsuko edged herself behind some of the standing riders to hide from him. She wanted to get up and move to the next car but didn't, thinking that this would attract his attention—which she didn't want.

It must be close to ten years now since Katchan had begun

to be a regular guest at her home. This was when Tatsuko was still attending junior college. She had taken her Akita dog named Kagetora with her shopping in the early evening, and the dog had pulled some squid off a plate in a shopfront, scattering it all over the road. Tatsuko scolded the dog and apologized to the proprietress and her young assistant. This young man obviously liked dogs. "You're going to have a stomachache if you eat squid like that," he declared, and tossed Kagetora a piece of mackerel. The dog was not entirely trained and promptly swallowed the whole piece before Tatsuko could stop him. She thanked the proprietress and the assistant, apologizing profusely, and hauled the dog back home.

One street from the house, Kagetora collapsed on his hind legs and began groaning. No matter how Tatsuko coaxed him, he wouldn't move and soon began to foam at the mouth. Tatsuko managed to get him home with the neighbors' help, but she couldn't just do nothing about his distressed condition. Tying the dog to a wisteria trellis, she called a veterinarian. After receiving a few injections, Kagetora vomited a partially digested piece of fish, in the center of which was a globefish the size of a toy car.

Later that evening, the young shop assistant came to apologize, since Tatsuko's father had telephoned the fish shop to tell them what had happened. Kagetora had recovered fully as soon as he spit up the globefish, and Tatsuko's father felt there was no need to take the matter further, as the whole episode had been started by the dog. But he decided it was advisable to let the shop know what had happened in any case. The young fellow apologized, bowing so deeply that he almost touched the ground. The proprietress herself would have come, he said, but her husband was in poor health. He offered, as a sign of their sincere regret, an enormous sole in a basket.

The middle-aged couple owned the Uotomi Fish Shop together, but the husband had developed a kidney problem. The
only thing he did was slice raw fish for sashimi. The rest of the
time he would sit at the entryway to the living quarters in the
rear of the shop and watch the street, his face pale and swollen,
a cigarette in his hand. Before long he had become bedridden
upstairs, and the young man began to work at the shop.

Said to be related to the shopkeeper's wife, the assistant was
tall and very good looking. When Tatsuko found him standing at
the entryway to her house wearing an expensive bomber jacket
instead of the huge rubber-lined apron over his work clothes,
she had mistaken him for a friend of her older brother, a university student. Apologizing repeatedly for the incident, the assistant finally took his leave. As Tatsuko was locking the front door,
she overheard a loud voice saying, "I'm so sorry." Peering outside, she saw the man kneeling down on the grass in front of
Kagetora's doghouse and apologizing to the dog. She had felt
this was going too far, she recalled.

This young man was Katchan.

Katchan began coming to Tatsuko's house virtually every
day, bringing pieces of whitefish for Kagetora to eat. His excuse
to Tatsuko and her mother was that the fish was a leftover and,
besides, he wanted to do it. "Don't worry. I've taken the bones
out." He made a point of showing Tatsuko the cleaned fish.

An animal is an animal by nature. Kagetora quickly became
attached to Katchan, and as soon as he saw him holding an old
kerosene can with fish leftovers, he wagged his bushy tail. The
tail hitting the clapboard walls of the doghouse could be heard
even from inside the house. Within less than two weeks after
the incident, Katchan had assumed the responsibility of taking
Kagetora out for exercise.

Kagetora had come from a friend of Tatsuko's older brother. He had been as small as a cat, but had grown quickly into a large dog. Brushing him and taking him out for a walk was no easy task for Tatsuko. Her brother, who had said he would look after the dog, had half-moved out of their house to be with his girlfriend, a fellow university student, and was often not at home. The care of the dog was eventually left to Tatsuko and her mother. To be honest, the dog was too big for them to handle and had become a nuisance. After Katchan began to look after Kagetora, however, his fur became surprisingly lustrous, perhaps because of all the feeding and brushing. The cost of his food, which Tatsuko's mother had occasionally grumbled about, was now of small concern since Katchan brought fish every day.

Tatsuko's mother offered some money to Katchan for his help and suggested that he buy himself a shirt or something, but Katchan said he would spend it on building Kagetora a bigger doghouse. The one they had was the cheapest one made and had been bought when Kagetora was still small, since they had not expected the dog to grow so big; now it was too cramped for him. Refusing to go in the doghouse, Kagetora stayed outside, even in the rain.

Katchan spent one whole Sunday shopping for lumber and paint and then building a new doghouse. When Tatsuko came home at dusk with a tennis racket under her arm, there beside the entrance to the house was a huge doghouse, so large she began to laugh. She was immediately shocked to see Kagetora tied to the gatepost with blood around his mouth. It turned out to be red paint, however, not blood. No doubt Kagetora had touched the red roof of the doghouse while playing with Katchan when he was painting.

Katchan was invited into the house for dinner with the family for the first time that evening—father, mother, and Tatsuko only, for her brother didn't come home. Tatsuko's mother took care to serve a meat dish, sukiyaki, saying that Katchan was probably tired of fish. Katchan took over the role of host, cooking the sukiyaki at the table, serving beer to Tatsuko's father, and joking with everyone to make them laugh. Tatsuko's father, who was much less talkative now that his son had moved out of the home, laughed loudly, exposing his white teeth.

Katchan was quite loquacious. Uotomi's proprietor had been told he wouldn't live long. He and his wife had no children and wanted to adopt Katchan as a son so he could inherit the shop, but Katchan hadn't made up his mind yet.

"I wish fish didn't have faces. They have faces and eyes, you know. In the beginning I dreaded cutting into them," Katchan said.

"In the beginning there was no such thing as precut fish!" the father joked.

The Uotomi Fish Shop had been in the family for three generations. They also owned two rental houses behind the shop. If they were to demolish the houses and put up an apartment in their place, the rent alone would be enough for them to live on. Considering the future of the fish shop, which was bound to be driven out of business by the fish department of some big supermarket, Katchan thought of opening up a nice little place on his own. "Would a coffee shop do, I wonder, or would a snack bar be better?" he asked, looking into Tatsuko's eyes.

The sukiyaki dinner was over, and after they had finished dessert—watermelon—Katchan stayed on for a bit. He explained how to tell the difference between flatfish and sole, and mimicked the leatherfish, which makes a squeaking sound, like new shoes. He talked nonstop as if scared that the conversation would die and the evening be over, and he smoked as if he knew that as long as there was a lighted cigarette he wouldn't be told,

"Well, then, time to go home." When Katchan lit a cigarette he was smiling, but he looked ready to cry.

Katchan talked about the "dog map." He had heard that each dog had a map of its own, totally different from what humans thought of as a map. The dog map was a mental map of the neighborhood that each dog carried around in its head showing the various landmarks—the house with the tormenting brat, another where he could get scraps of meat, another where his favorite bitch lived, which telephone poles and hedges were part of his territory, and so on. Tatsuko's father, who usually went to bed early, yawned, and her mother took that as a sign to leave the table to make up his bed for him. At last Katchan went home.

"A dog map, is it?" Tatsuko's mother muttered.

"He's talking about himself, I suppose," Tatsuko's father said. He seemed to know Katchan very well.

From the next day, Katchan began entering Tatsuko's house through the back kitchen door, as if he were entitled to the place.

"Give me a pot, a very large pot, please," he requested, putting the fish he had brought with him into the pot and beginning to cook it himself. The odor of fish spread through the house. Katchan took Kagetora out for his walk while the fish was cooking. When he returned, he brushed the dog thoroughly, fed it, placed the leftovers in a Tupperware bowl, stored the food in the refrigerator, and then went back home. He appeared quite accustomed to these tasks, as if he had been doing them for years.

Tatsuko's brother came home to pick up his clean underwear. "Hey, you've got a different smell," he said to Kagetora. "You smell like fish." When Kagetora put his black pointed nose up to his cheek to lick it, the brother pushed it away, averting his face. The family hadn't noticed the smell because fish for them had become a daily occurrence. Before Katchan, the dog had eaten meat, too. When the brother heard about Katchan, he smiled at Tatsuko and said jokingly, "Well, you've found yourself a man." He left carrying off more belongings than usual. He could be more open now that Tatsuko had a man.

Katchan was a handy person to have around the house. He hauled away the big pine branch that had broken off in the typhoon, and he fixed the fallen tiles around the bathtub. He began to call Tatsuko's father "Dad" and her mother "Mom," and even called Tatsuko "Tatchan," the endearment her mother used.

Watermelon began to appear in the shops again. It was now one year since Kagetora had swallowed the mackerel and made all that fuss. Tatsuko's parents had gone off to a family wedding, leaving Tatsuko alone in the house for the night. The house was old, having survived the bombings during the war, and it stood on a large piece of land. Tatsuko wanted her older brother to come home to stay with her and tried to contact him. But his girlfriend must not have given him the message, for he didn't come around.

It must have been after nine o'clock when Katchan came to take Kagetora out for his walk after he had closed up the fish shop and had dinner. As usual, the smell of cooking fish permeated the house. Tatsuko could hear Kagetora's now thickened tail slap-slapping the doghouse wall, showing the dog's affection for Katchan. "He takes twice as long to brush the dog when you're around," her mother had observed, and Tatsuko felt a bit annoyed. She heard Katchan's voice as he left with Kagetora. He was whistling, possibly the theme music from a foreign movie;

perhaps he had learned it for her to hear. Katchan had called out that they were leaving, but she had pretended not to hear. After watching from the window as Katchan and Kagetora went off, Tatsuko took a shower to get rid of the fish odor that seemed to cling to her. If Katchan cycles around the park and throws balls for Kagetora to catch, it should take an hour or so, she thought. Tatsuko put on a dressing gown and watched TV in the dining room, sipping wine from a bottle her father had opened.

Tatsuko must have dozed off without realizing it, for she woke up when Kagetora jumped on her. "How did you get in the house?" she muttered, still in a dozy stupor, pushing away the dog and brushing aside its warm tongue that was licking around her mouth. "You smell like fish," she said. Then she realized that it was not Kagetora but Katchan.

"Forgive me," Katchan said, still clinging to her. Tatsuko couldn't recall how or when she finally got rid of him. When she came to her senses, the wine glass was shattered on the floor.

Her body ached all over the following morning, and she had bruises on her elbows and knees. She walked to the gate to pick up the morning paper as her father did every morning. Emerging from his doghouse, Kagetora wagged his tail. It wasn't his fault, but recalling the previous night's incident, Tatsuko didn't feel like looking at him. But as she turned her face away, she noticed flecks of something around his mouth. "Don't chew the paint off the roof," she scolded, then realized that it wasn't paint. This time it was dried blood. Wondering if the dog had killed a cat, Tatsuko looked inside the doghouse. Aghast, she saw the feet of a man wearing a pair of sneakers.

Lying in the oversized doghouse, Katchan was sound asleep, snoring loudly. Perhaps he'd been drinking out of desperation and had slept in the doghouse. I won't wake him up—why should I? thought Tatsuko, and spun around to reenter the house. As she did, she spied an empty bottle of sleeping pills at Katchan's feet. She froze. Katchan had gone to a late-night supermarket, bought the pills, and tried to kill himself.

The blood on Kagetora's mouth was from an injury the dog had caused when it playfully bit Katchan in an attempt to wake him up—or so it turned out. Thanks to the small amount of pills and the occasional nudge by Kagetora, Katchan was all right, and he left for his home in the countryside three days later. Tatsuko didn't say a word to her parents. They seemed to sense what had happened.

After Katchan left, Kagetora's fur quickly lost its luster. Tatsuko had an arranged meeting at the end of the year with a man, her present husband, who at the time was a resident anesthetist. One of the main reasons she decided to marry him was the smell of antiseptic solution that clung to him.

Before the next cherry blossom season, the owner of the Uotomi Fish Shop died and the shop was closed. Tatsuko found out there had never been any talk of taking Katchan as the adopted son. The shop was demolished along with several adjacent shops and now a new building stood in their place. Kagetora had died of distemper two years later. Looking back now, that enormously big doghouse was Katchan himself, perhaps.

Tatsuko thought she could have spoken to him had she not been pregnant. The train arrived at the station where Tatsuko had to transfer. She saw, between the legs of the standing passengers, the family—the couple and their son—still deeply asleep, all bent double, Katchan's hands firmly holding onto the oversize camera so it couldn't slip away.

The Fake Egg

WHEN SACHIKO WOKE UP, THE FIRST THING SHE DID WAS GO to the kitchen and take two eggs out of the refrigerator. It was her morning ritual. She put them out in a bowl and then went to brush her teeth and wash her face. Eggs straight out of the refrigerator didn't taste good, and she had been told that they would cook better when left for a while at room temperature.

The ice-cold eggs seemed stiff and leaden. They bumped against each other, making a dull clunk in the white bowl, but soon they stopped moving.

It would be so much easier if her husband Takeo would just have toast and coffee for breakfast, but he always said he didn't feel he had really eaten breakfast unless it was a Japanese-style one with rice.

"I'll have toast and coffee after our child is born," Takeo had promised Sachiko on their honeymoon.

Sachiko thought then that her rice-cooking period would be only a year or so long at most. It never occurred to her that it might last five years.

"Not ready yet?" Takeo asked her at the table, the morning paper spread before him. He had forgotten about a morning conference and wanted Sachiko to hurry up with his breakfast.

The phrase "not ready yet" was the last thing Sachiko wanted to hear.

"Not ready yet?"

"Don't you think it's about time?" her mother-in-law had asked Sachiko more than once.

Sachiko was thankful she wasn't living with her in-laws. Takeo was an only child, and his mother was awaiting the birth of his heir. After waiting three years, though, she avoided raising the question of children when she met Sachiko. Sachiko would have preferred to be asked openly about it than to have the subject ignored.

Takeo left it to Sachiko to crack open the eggs at the breakfast table. The eggs were warmer now than they had been in the refrigerator but still colder than the white bowl. The egg whites looked half-transparent and half-frozen, perhaps because she had lowered the refrigerator temperature to make sherbet. She whisked Takeo's egg more vigorously than usual and added some soy sauce for flavor. When she broke her own egg into a bowl she cried out; there was a spot of blood on the white.

"What's the matter?" Takeo asked, peering out from behind the barricade of his morning paper. He seemed disappointed. "It's nothing. Just take the bloody part out." He offered to eat Sachiko's egg but she had now lost her appetite for it.

"Sometimes eggs are kind of disgusting," said Sachiko. "Once, when I was a child, I broke open an egg and out came what was almost a baby chick." Sachiko took her egg to the kitchen, half concealing it from her husband, and put some seaweed preserves on top of the rice in her rice bowl. The unborn bird had had a whitish beak and huge eyes for the size of its body. The revulsion still lingered, and every time Sachiko cracked open an egg she remembered the chick.

"You don't know anything, do you?" Takeo looked at her incredulously. His lips and the area around his mouth were yellow from eating the raw egg and rice. "There is no chance of getting an egg like that any more."

"Why not?" asked Sachiko.

"Nowadays they're all unfertilized."

"How can they be 'unfertilized'?" Sachiko almost asked, then swallowed her words.

There was silence for a while.

"Eggs don't come from country farms any more. So roosters and hens don't peck at their food together in farmyards. Roosters get turned into grill meat and hens are lined up in cages and forced to eat and lay eggs. That's all they do."

Sachiko wanted to ask if some hens produced unfertilized eggs even when they were with roosters, but stopped. She had sensed something in Takeo's voice when he began to speak again after the silence—a casualness, a pretended casualness. Takeo always said that they shouldn't hurry to have a family. And if they weren't able to have children, then they simply wouldn't have any. He had refused Sachiko's suggestion that they should both have a medical check-up.

The chill of the eggs made Sachiko recall a scene at a china shop near her elementary school. She vaguely remembered she was with her mother, who had come to meet her. Beneath some shelves laden with rice bowls and tea cups was a large earthenware dish containing many eggs. She had picked one of the eggs up and had been surprised at how cold and heavy it was. She was told it was a fake egg made of porcelain, called a "waterglass egg." Some hens laid their eggs under houses or in other odd places, and the waterglass eggs were used to show the hens the proper places to lay. They could also be used to get a hen to sit on the eggs of another hen. Sachiko considered her love life with

Takeo very good. But because she couldn't bear children, however often they made love, she felt her body must be made of
porcelain, like the waterglass eggs.

After dinner Hideko, Sachiko's high school friend, came to
visit. She was a year older than Sachiko, almost thirty, and had
not yet married. She worked in advertising. She already smelled
of alcohol when she arrived but wanted more to drink. So Takeo
shared several whiskey and waters with her.

"Are you all right?" Sachiko asked. Hideko was tossing her
drinks back like a man, unusual for her.

"It's one last fling. I'm drinking because I have to go on the
wagon for a while, starting tomorrow." Hideko laughed, but it
was clear she was trying to hide her real feelings. "I messed up."
Hideko shrugged.

Sachiko guessed she meant she had gotten herself pregnant.

"I'm seeing the doctor tomorrow afternoon to take care of
the problem, but I need a person to contact in case anything
happens to me. I live with my parents, but I can't give their
names. Would it be OK if I gave them your name instead?"
asked Hideko, pressing her hands together as if in prayer.

"It's weird, isn't it? Children aren't born where they're badly
wanted, and those who don't want them get pregnant," Sachiko
said.

"It's like the lottery," Hideko agreed. "The person who has
everything draws the winning ticket."

"That's a strange comparison," Sachiko laughed, noticing an
unusual expression in Takeo's eyes, which were fixed on
Hideko's body. Hideko came to see them every three months or
so, but now that Takeo knew she was pregnant, he was looking
at her as if meeting her for the first time. His eyes shone warmly.

"Well, maybe you two could raise my child," Hideko said.

"Thanks, but if we adopt a child we'd rather have one we don't know anything about," Sachiko said without thinking. "Besides, if there was something wrong with the child, I would hate you, and if the child was perfect, then you would want it back for yourself."

"Hmm, that's a thought." Hideko nodded.

Helping himself to more whiskey, Takeo was silent.

The following day, Sachiko went to the university medical school hospital without telling Takeo. She had to know once and for all whether she could have children. If the examination showed she couldn't, she was prepared to accept the verdict. But she couldn't take not knowing any longer. The doctors said it would take two weeks to get the results.

Sachiko was afraid the smell of the antiseptic lingered on her body. It was as if she'd snuck off to the hospital to have a love affair, and was now on her guard so that no one would guess she had been there.

The examination revealed that Sachiko was capable of conceiving. Her reproductive organs may have been a little underdeveloped, but all was well, the doctor said. So, I'm not a waterglass egg, not that cold, hard, porcelain egg but a warm, human egg. She was pleased, but she was also upset about past events. For years she had had to hang her head in shame at family gatherings with Takeo, feeling inadequate because she had not yet had a baby. Her mother-in-law and the other relatives spoke as if *she* were solely responsible. But I'm not responsible, Sachiko thought; if anything, the fault is with Takeo. Could it be that he knew he was the culprit all along?

"You know a man can have mumps without even knowing it. It's unfair that I'm the one who's blamed. Please have yourself looked at," Sachiko begged.

"I can get a woman pregnant," Takeo said.

"Have you had an examination?"

"No, not exactly," said Takeo. Then, reluctantly—he hadn't really wanted her to know this—he confessed that before they married, he'd had an affair with a woman who had conceived his child.

"But anyway, the child was never born."

"Who was she?" asked Sachiko.

Takeo stretched out his hand for a cigarette.

In her five years of marriage, Sachiko had learned that men smoke when they don't want to talk. They put a stop to things by puffing out smoke instead of words.

"I won't ask her name then. But is it really true?" asked Sachiko.

Through the billow of smoke, he nodded.

Takeo's face was hardly apologetic; it seemed to be boasting that it was not his fault.

In the early evening of the following day, Sachiko got off at Higashi Nakano on Tokyo's Chuo Line and climbed the narrow slope in front of the station. After much hesitation, she had made up her mind to come. Her destination was a small bar called The Drop. It had no booths and was so small that the counter and ten patrons on bar stools would completely fill the place. Takeo had once taken her there, saying he had been a good customer since his university days. The mama-san of the bar was a thin, tough-looking woman with long, unpermed hair. She was probably a few years older than Takeo. When Takeo introduced Sachiko as his fiancee, she broke into a smile.

"Congratulations!" she said, banging a glass of Campari and soda on the counter. "That's great. Really great," she repeated. "I'll have a drink tonight. It's your treat, Takeo."

She acted excited, but Sachiko sensed that she was forcing herself. The way she put the glass down on the counter betrayed her. Sachiko had forgotten all about her until she heard Takeo's confession, but then she suddenly recalled the mama-san. If he was telling the truth, then the pregnant woman had to be her, Sachiko thought, although she had no grounds for her suspicion.

The Drop was still in the same location. Its name was the same but the place had been remodeled, and the sign protruding above the sidewalk looked different. Sachiko pushed the door open. There was no trace of the intimate bar of five years ago; it was more like a typical cocktail lounge now. The young bartender slicing a lemon told her that the present manager had bought the place three years ago. He knew nothing of the mama-san under the previous manager.

Reluctant to leave, Sachiko ordered a glass of whiskey and water. There were no other customers in the bar. She sat near the window and looked outside. What would she have said to the mama-san had she been there? "Is it true you carried his child?" or "Are you sure the baby was his? Couldn't the father have been someone else?" Sachiko repeated the questions she probably couldn't have brought herself to ask anyway.

The Chuo Line rumbled just below. "I'm not blaming you. I came on the scene after you and I have no right to blame you. I just want to know the truth," Sachiko wanted to tell the woman. She couldn't bear to spend the rest of her life wavering between doubt and belief, blaming Takeo for her barrenness. She wanted to make it clear once and for all. The train passed again.

Suddenly someone spoke: "I've just taken your photo. You looked so nice and I knew I shouldn't, but—" It was a man in his early thirties, about Takeo's age.

"Can I send you the pictures when they're ready?" he asked. The man's camera wasn't at all like Takeo's; it was substantial and heavy. Noticing the way he handled his camera and his clothes, which looked rather like U.S. Army camouflage, Sachiko guessed he was a professional photographer.

"Don't think I'm bragging, but I think I did very well with this shot. I have a hunch I did. Do you mind if I send the prints to you?"

Sachiko thought that photos taken of her in this particular bar were not a very good idea. Had they been in some other bar, it might have been all right.

Seeing Sachiko hesitate, the photographer said, "Well then, let's do this." He fished a large datebook from his khaki camera bag, muttering, "Schedule, schedule, where are you?" and leafed through its pages. Each day was divided into several sections, with appointments written in. He had to be a professional.

"How about if I bring them for you here at the same time a week from today?" he asked.

Sachiko took this bold suggestion in. Perhaps it was the easy way he said it, but she unconsciously nodded in agreement.

When she woke up the next day, Sachiko went immediately to the kitchen and took two eggs from the refrigerator. The cold eggs shivered and clicked against each other as if alive, but then became still, looking like a married couple. These were not real eggs, but some sort of egglike things. Even heated up, the two could not produce a child and become a family. Takeo and Sachiko probably had consumed a few thousand eggs for breakfast since they got married. But they only ate eggs; they couldn't produce them. Sachiko had kept her visit to The Drop a secret, and now she felt as if some translucent wall had come between her and her husband. Sachiko wasn't quite sure that Takeo's confession was true. Yet her spirits were up. She wondered if this was because she was looking forward to seeing the photos.

Sachiko returned to The Drop a week later. The photographer was already there. He handed her the photos without a word. The woman in the photos resembled her, but Sachiko felt she was looking at a stranger. In some of the photos her eyes were closed. In others, her eyes were half-opened, her unfocused gaze directed upward. In another, she was frowning as if in pain, creating a deep wrinkle between her eyebrows. In all the black-and-white five-by-eights, her lips were partly opened. Sachiko never knew she had such facial expressions. She was embarrassed; her cheeks were burning. How could she have looked like this when she had been thinking about such a difficult problem—the relationship between Takeo and the mama-san of the bar? The photos revealed an unexpected sensuality.

The man peered into Sachiko's eyes and lit a cigarette. "Your face looking at the photos is the same as the face in the photos. That's interesting," he said.

Sachiko blushed again. She was afraid to look at the man, so she fixed her gaze on his fingers holding the cigarette. They were long, thick fingers that tapered at the ends, just like Takeo's, very artistic looking. The thumbs were stubby with square, short fingernails, like Takeo's as well. One time years before, when Sachiko and her mother were warming their hands in front of the heater, Sachiko had noticed how her own fingers and the shape of her nails were very similar to those of her mother. Now her eyes automatically went to the hands every time she met a stranger. Perhaps fingers had some correlation with height. The man, who was tall and thin, probably suffered from indigestion like Takeo, she thought.

"How many children do you have?" Sachiko asked, before she knew what she was saying.

"That's an interesting question," he laughed, looking into her eyes. "Just one. Do you mean to say that a man with a child is no good to you?"

Sachiko wanted to close her eyes. "Oh, no. It's completely the opposite," she wanted to say. Her question had been unmistakable: Can you get a woman pregnant? She didn't want to break up her marriage. She needed a child to strengthen her marriage. She had no intention of using the photographer to get a child. But she had asked him whether he had children. Did she have emotions and intentions she wasn't aware of herself, just as she had faces she never imagined she possessed?

"Shall we leave?" The man's long fingers picked up the bill.

Sachiko walked slowly beside the photographer down the narrow slope along the railway track. The trains on the Chuo Line passed in both directions, packed with people in the evening rush hour.

The man suddenly stopped walking. "Scissors-stone-paper," he invited, gesturing with his hand. "If I win, let's go in here." They stood in front of a love hotel.

Tongue-tied, Sachiko just stood there.

"Ready? One-two—"

Tempted by his gesture, she held her hand ready.

Three, Sachiko thought to herself, suddenly running off. Without looking back, she ran straight for Higashi Nakano Station.

A month later, Sachiko discovered she was pregnant. A doctor assured her it was true. She had not even held his hand, but she believed the photographer had to be the child's father. Her marriage to Takeo had not been a love match; an old friend had introduced them. She was not unhappy in her marriage, but she had never experienced burning passion either. To get pregnant, did she have to have both her emotions and her body warmed up first—like eggs?

Sachiko took the photos from the bottom of her underwear drawer and looked at her eyes half-closed in abandonment. Her face in pain, with the deep wrinkle between her eyebrows. Her lips half-parted as if waiting to receive something. This is the exact moment I became pregnant. What should I do with these photos? Tear them to shreds and throw them away? Should I burn them to ashes?

Deliberating, Sachiko dialed the number of Takeo's company; she wanted him to be the first to know. But the line was busy. Before I speak to him, I have to make up my mind about what to do with the photos. Should I throw them away, or what?

"Sorry to keep you waiting. I'll put you through now," the operator's voice said, but the extension kept ringing. Sachiko thought she would keep the photos. She was certain she would never tell Takeo about them. They would remain hidden beneath her lingerie in the chest of drawers.

"Hello." Takeo's voice sounded very dear.

"Hello," Sachiko said, but she couldn't go on. Her eyes were filling with tears.

Triangular Chop

TWO PIGEONS PERCHED ON A POWER LINE. THE FIRST HAD dropped down onto the line. The other had settled beside it, leaving enough distance for another to alight. The line swayed faintly and the two birds adjusted themselves to the movement. When the line became still, one began to preen itself.

They're a pair, Makiko thought. She looked down, her forehead pressed to the glass window. The one preening itself looked smaller than the other, but a bit chubbier.

The window was in the ladies room on the fifth floor of the company where Makiko worked, and the scene across the street was a familiar one: high-rise securities companies and office buildings, crowding tall as if to crush the Security Exchange on the left, while in the caverns below, small one-story houses held their ground. In this season of blue skies and tall, puffy clouds, Tokyo was enshrouded in heavy, gray smog. Dismal though the scene was, Makiko felt lighthearted as she looked to the future. This was the last time she would gaze out on this view. She must have come to this spot at least three or four times a day during the three years she had worked for the company, but she had never noticed the power lines just below the window and the pigeons coming to perch on them. Makiko kept staring out, wondering if there were other opportunities she had missed.

Her last day at the company had been the day before; her colleagues had given her a farewell party, and in tears she had left them, holding hands to the melody of "Auld Lang Syne." It was embarrassing to visit the company again today to fill out the form for unemployment benefits.

"Ah, it's you. You've come in again?" someone called to her.

"I really hate this sort of situation. It's like saying goodbye to everyone at the railway station, but then the train doesn't leave," Makiko said.

She had asked her former coworkers not to come and see her off on her honeymoon. The wedding was scheduled for the following day.

The two pigeons were still on the line, apart. Makiko thought they should be closer, and laughed. The two birds were just like she and Tatsuo. He used to ask her to go to a hotel room once a week, but since they had set the wedding date, he went straight home after dinner or tea. Makiko could understand, in her head, that he had wanted to make a formal new beginning, but in her heart she felt a bit lonely.

Tatsuo liked things prim and proper.

"He'd look better in an army uniform than a suit," her grandmother had said when Makiko brought him to her home.

Tatsuo wasn't very tall, but he was very polite and sturdy, probably the result of his kendo practice.

"Yes, sir!" he would snap smartly and give a quick, deep bow. Makiko's grandmother nicknamed him "the chrysanthemum doll" for the warrior figures made entirely of chrysanthemum petals and seen at exhibitions.

A new pigeon swooped down and perched next to the one that was preening. The line swayed to and fro, as if the three birds were on a swing. The new pigeon, using the momentum of the swing, flew up a bit and mounted the one that was preening itself. Makiko averted her gaze. Were the birds mating? She'd seen the words "mating season" in her almanac, but for city birds it really didn't apply, did it? The power line swung back and forth, and the two mating pigeons swayed with the movement. Just when Makiko felt she could hardly breathe, the pigeon on top flew away, followed by the lower one. A few gray feathers floated down slowly from the wire. The one pigeon perched apart from its mate remained motionless; it did not look around.

Makiko knew she was blushing. The deserted pigeon was Tatsuo, whom she was going to marry the following day. The preener was Makiko. The newcomer was Hatano, a junior staff member in Tatsuo's section. This at least was how it seemed to Makiko.

"Anything worrying you?" a voice asked. It was Kayoko, Makiko's senior in the company by two years.

Makiko replied that she wasn't worrying; she just missed the company. Looking right into Makiko's eyes, Kayoko retorted that she couldn't exactly miss the company while standing by a window in the ladies room; the shape of Makiko's back had told her something was wrong. At that moment Makiko decided to tell Kayoko what was worrying her. Kayoko had been correct. Makiko did have something on her mind, but it wasn't serious; it was the kind of problem that doubles the happiness of a young woman about to be married.

Makiko arranged to meet Kayoko at the coffee shop in the basement of the building. She took another look out the window. The pigeon had gone.

"He's my fiance's subordinate. I won't tell you his name, but I think he loves me," Makiko said to Kayoko. Once she had revealed this much, the rest was as easy as unraveling a sweater.

The man, Hatano, had begun to come between Makiko and Tatsuo soon after their wedding plans were finalized. Before that Tatsuo had been using Hatano as his chauffeur. If the two were out on a date and it suddenly began raining, or if they couldn't find a taxi after a movie, Tatsuo would telephone Hatano to come and pick them up. Hatano always came, driving his immaculate car. He was a well-dressed, seemingly well-bred young man, always pleasant, never showing a sign of annoyance.

He was polite to Makiko, his superior's girlfriend, opening and closing the car door for her as if he were a real chauffeur and Makiko his mistress. Makiko was embarrassed, but Tatsuo took it for granted. He didn't thank him, and he let Hatano go home without even treating him to a cup of coffee.

Tatsuo in fact was hard on Hatano. He complained, for instance, that Hatano was late or had come to the wrong place. Makiko, unable to bear it, began to defend Hatano, but Tatsuo would say, "Never mind. Don't worry. I've done enough for him." Tatsuo seemed to be saying that Hatano's errands were well compensated for at work, and Hatano himself didn't seem to mind Tatsuo's complaints.

"The boss always scolds me," said Hatano, turning in the driver's seat to face Makiko, giving her a soft smile.

Tatsuo scolded his smiling face. "You blinked again. I've told you time and again not to blink." Tatsuo believed that blinking in a man was a sign of cowardice, giving the impression he was unreliable and not a good securities dealer.

"He even comments on your blinking! Life isn't easy for you, is it?" Makiko said to Hatano. Looking at his long eyelashes, she sympathized with him. Tatsuo, a pragmatist, probably figured that as long as a person had eyeballs, that was enough. His own lashes were thin and sparse.

The two men were complete opposites. Tatsuo was highly

regarded by his colleagues and had become a chief clerk before
he was thirty, whereas Hatano, three years his junior, had gotten
a job with the company through an influential relative, and his
private life seemed more important to him than excelling at his
work. Tatsuo was a drinker, and he was proud that he never got
really drunk. One weekend, on the way home after a date with
Makiko, he had dozed off in the car after having some drinks.
He had had an exhausting week at work. When Tatsuo began to
snore, Hatano, in the driver's seat, turned on the car radio and
began to chat with Makiko, who was feeling bored. Hatano had
a sensitivity that Tatsuo didn't possess, and Makiko enjoyed
talking with him. When Tatsuo woke up, she secretly wished he
had slept longer.

It was at the time of the engagement that Makiko had
sensed Hatano's feelings. Looking straight ahead, with a frozen
expression on his face, he had barely glanced at Makiko when
offering his congratulations. Normally polite when closing the
car door, he had slammed it shut on this occasion.

"Is that all?" Kayoko laughed, playing with an empty coffee
cup. "He's single, isn't he? Then it's quite natural for him to
behave that way. It's your fault. You shouldn't have used a young
bachelor as a chauffeur for your dates."

Makiko wasn't happy with Kayoko's response. "If it was just
jealousy or being upset, then surely he'd have quit as chauffeur
after our engagement, but he still continues. Not only that, he
seems to be around more than ever. Several times when we've
left a movie theater his car has been waiting."

Kayoko put a cigarette in her mouth and lit it. She wanted to
strike a pose with the cigarette, but if she inhaled deeply she
would cough, Makiko knew.

"When he looks at me, his eyes are different. He stares at

me with those eyes. They pierce right through me. When we were moving furniture into the new house, he insisted on helping us—and did a great job," said Makiko.

"Well, your fiance's his boss. He'd want to stay on his good side. That's the hard part about being white collar," Kayoko said.

"Oh, I don't think that's it," Makiko said.

Makiko gave some further examples. She told Kayoko of the time they had gone to a department store to select the small gifts they were obliged to give their wedding guests. When Makiko arrived at the store on her lunch break, Tatsuo was there as arranged—but with Hatano. And Hatano had uncharacteristically insisted on a set of silver spoons he had taken a liking to. "Usually he's pretty reserved and modest, but here he was acting like the bridegroom himself. Maybe he wanted to participate in the event somehow."

Kayoko said nothing.

If only Kayoko would say, "He's in love with you because you're attractive," then Makiko would stop talking. Makiko had often been told she was not sentimental like a woman but behaved more like a man because of all the hardship she had been through, and she had never been described as beautiful or feminine. She imagined that Tatsuo had chosen her because she was bright and healthy, had few relatives, and would be an asset to him. So she wanted to hear the words she had ached to hear for so long—"Because you're attractive"—and then go home.

"The other night it was horrible. Tatsuo and I were in the back seat as usual when Hatano suddenly sped up. He almost collided with an oncoming car," she said.

Tatsuo, who had been dozing on and off, got upset and cried out, "Hey, careful! I'm not ready for a love-suicide."

"A love-suicide takes two people, not three," said Hatano in a low voice without looking back.

Kayoko puffed out a cloud of smoke. "No wonder there's no man for me; this woman has two for herself!"

At last Makiko had heard what she was waiting for. The real reason Makiko had decided to marry Tatsuo was her age—she was twenty-four. She certainly loved Tatsuo, but she knew he lacked finesse and sensitivity. In her heart of hearts she was toting up his money and future prospects. But that was too miserable a reason to lose her single life, so she had colored the story of Hatano by telling Kayoko that he was a good deal more handsome than he really was.

Kayoko pressed her cigarette butt into an ashtray with a big sigh, and Makiko added another tidbit.

The night before last, Makiko had gone to see Tatsuo at his office after work to discuss details of the wedding ceremony. Only Tatsuo and Hatano were left in the vast office. Tatsuo had been staying late since he was going to take three days off for his honeymoon and had to finish his work before he left.

When Tatsuo stepped out to buy a pack of cigarettes, Hatano, until then working in silence, suddenly said with a lopsided smile, "Women are really something, aren't they? Even if they know something, they pretend not to." The comment was so sudden that Makiko couldn't answer. Groping for words, she heard Tatsuo's footsteps. That was all.

"What would you do if Hatano asked you to marry him?" Kayoko asked Makiko, as expected.

"I'd be very flattered, but I think I'd refuse him. You know I would," said Makiko.

Makiko went home without telling Kayoko about the scene she had witnessed, in which the female pigeon had flown away with a new mate.

There were some other things she had left out because they

weren't directly related to her main point. For example, the evening she had visited Tatsuo at his office, Tatsuo wanted to have a smoke and had first taken a pack of cigarettes out of his own pocket. But the pack was empty. Tatsuo fumbled in his pocket for change but could find none. Hatano at the time was making photocopies, leaning over the machine, with his back toward them. Tatsuo went over and pulled out the wallet that was protruding from Hatano's back-trouser pocket and walked out into the corridor to the vending machine. Makiko felt Tatsuo should at least have said, "I'm borrowing some small change," but then Hatano began to make his comment about women. Even a close friend should have a minimum of manners, Makiko thought.

There was another thing Makiko didn't tell Kayoko. Every time Makiko looked at a newspaper or magazine, the three characters that made up "Hatano" jumped out before her eyes as if printed in heavy boldface type. For instance, this morning, when she had opened the daily paper, the character *ha*, for "waves," caught her attention. "Can the mystery of the cruel sea be solved?" was the headline. At Nojimazaki, off Chiba Prefecture, many large mineral-carrying freighters had been torn apart or lost at sea in the past ten years. All had been caught in rough waves—a "triangular chop"—and had had their bows damaged, probably causing their shipwreck. Triangular chop. Makiko had heard the expression before and wondered what sort of wave it was. She had been surprised to find herself unconsciously looking for the character for "waves." Then she was startled again by the word "triangle." Perhaps the article in the morning paper had somehow been on her mind, and that was why she had thought of the three of them—Tatsuo, Hatano, and herself— when she had seen the three pigeons from the bathroom window. Since she had no parents to bid farewell to or who would shed tears for her, she might want to generate some youthful excitement by turning down one man to marry another. Makiko had never been happier, despite her confusion.

Hatano did not attend the wedding. Word was that he had a high fever and swollen tonsils. Makiko figured this was an excuse. Hatano couldn't bear to see her in her wedding dress. The reception was a great success, but Makiko felt that something was lacking.

Tatsuo was asleep, snoring in the bullet train en route to their honeymoon hotel. The junior members of his university kendo club had come to Tokyo Station and tossed him several times in the air. That'll sure make the alcohol circulate, Makiko thought. She looked out the window and saw herself reflected in the glass, wearing heavier make-up than usual. After she had put on her make-up and dressed in the white wedding gown, somewhere in her mind she had wanted Hatano to see her. Tatsuo was asleep with his mouth open as if he were sitting in a dentist's chair. When he put on an act he could look very confident, but his sleeping face seemed surprisingly childlike.

Makiko stared at the coarse oily skin on his chin where he had grazed himself while shaving. She gazed at his short stubby fingers and thick, hairy hands. I've put my life in those hands, Makiko thought. She tried to convince herself that Tatsuo was now her husband. He's an uncomplicated person, but he's not bad. I must give Hatano up, Makiko kept telling herself.

They arrived at the hotel in Shima and, after dinner, Tatsuo and Makiko played ping-pong. Tatsuo led a very ordered life and was usually in bed by 11:30 or midnight. He was no good at small talk and had gotten bored after dinner before they retired to their room. Although he had then suggested the ping-pong game, he wasn't very enthusiastic about playing and returned the ball feebly.

Totally different from the other occasion, Makiko thought. Tatsuo and Hatano had once played ping-pong at work, and Makiko had kept score. Tatsuo struck the ball hard, and Hatano smashed it back. When Tatsuo hit back again, he concentrated with all his might and, barely hiding his hostility, slammed the ball with all his strength. Hatano's pale face turned crimson. This wasn't a ping-pong game; it was more a fight with real swords. Hatano poured out his love for Makiko, and Tatsuo pushed it right back through his paddle. Intoxicated, Makiko felt she was watching the two men fighting a duel for her.

Soon bored with their uninspired game, Tatsuo and Makiko went back to their room. The telephone rang as if it had been waiting for their return. Makiko picked it up.

"Hello," she said.

There was silence for a moment, then, "This is Hatano." He spoke in his usual calm voice.

Makiko was speechless.

Tatsuo quickly took the receiver from her hand. "Is that you, Hatano? What a surprise!" Tatsuo spoke in a voice of forced calm.

Both men pretended to be unruffled. But they were hiding something. Hatano's telephone call was to seek Tatsuo's confirmation of some papers he had submitted to a client, or so he said, but for Makiko the call was clearly aimed at the time she and Tatsuo would be going to bed.

Tatsuo turned off the bedside light and stretched out his arm toward her. His action was nervous and awkward. Makiko also felt guilty because of the call and responded clumsily. It was even worse than the ping-pong game. Watching the dark ceiling with a heavy heart, Makiko felt as if Hatano were lying next to her in the double bed. Two pigeons perched apart. The third pigeon flew down next to the preening pigeon, and swinging on the line, mounted it, leaving a few feathers floating in the air. She recalled all this, as well as the gray, dismal city. The male pigeon who didn't protest at the new invader and allowed him to do whatever he wanted, that was Tatsuo, her husband lying next to her. Whether he was genuinely tolerant and liberal, and knew of Hatano's love for Makiko, or whether he truly thought that Hatano's call was about business, Makiko couldn't tell, because Tatsuo soon fell asleep with a snore.

Their new home, a rented house, was located in a suburb of Tokyo. A senior alumnus of Tatsuo's university had been transferred overseas soon after he'd bought the house, so for two years, until the man returned to Japan, Tatsuo and Makiko could live in the place at an exceptionally low rent. It took time to commute to work, but Tatsuo was pleased to have a house with a garden.

The first morning they moved into the house, Makiko went to open the wooden shutters. "I haven't had to open these things for years—not since I left my home in the country. I can't remember how to do it." She finally got one open and froze in horror. There, standing outside, was Hatano. He wasn't looking at Makiko. He was watching Tatsuo, who had gotten up and was standing behind Makiko. The morning paper in his hand, clad only in pajama trousers with no top, Tatsuo stood there speechless and motionless, like a chrysanthemum doll. Hatano uttered a muffled cry and sped away from the yard.

Suddenly everything switched and fell into place. It was Tatsuo that Hatano loved, not Makiko, as she had thought. The pigeon left all alone on the line was Makiko herself. The fierce fight the two men had had in the ping-pong game, smashing hard at each other's shots—the harder one hit the ball, the harder the other returned it—perhaps that was a kind of love. Hatano had been in the double bed all right, but he was there for Tatsuo and not for her.

"Have you ever heard of a 'triangular chop'?" Makiko asked Tatsuo, trying hard to disguise the tremble in her voice as she folded open the shutters.

"'Triangular chop'? Isn't that what happens when waves come at each other from opposite directions and pile up on each other? It's quite dangerous. It could even break a large ship in two. Doesn't it usually occur before a typhoon?"

Makiko felt a typhoon approaching.

"Do ships always sink in a triangular chop?" Makiko asked.

When she had finished folding open the four shutters, they had a full view of the garden. Houses just like theirs with white walls and red or blue roofs stood in rows.

"Not always, I think. I'm sure some ships manage to ride it out," Tatsuo said.

Tatsuo's hand came to rest on Makiko's shoulder. Should I brush it off, or trust the warmth on my shoulder and let it stay where it is? she wondered.

"Morning! Two bottles of milk for today, isn't it? I forgot them earlier and just popped back. I'll be more careful tomorrow. Sorry!" The cheery voice of the milkman called in from the kitchen door.

Mr. Carp

"SOMEONE'S HERE," WHISPERED MAYUMI, SHIOMURA'S DAUGHter. "The kitchen door just opened. I'm sure of it."

Shiomura didn't like this side of Mayumi. Her piano teacher had told her she had a good ear, so she had decided to enter a conservatory the year after next. Now she unabashedly flaunted her talent, whether to report on an alarm clock going off inside the house two doors away or on how the voice of a sweet potato vendor had changed. Whenever Shiomura said he didn't hear or couldn't tell the difference, Mayumi was blatantly scornful.

Her attitude made him stubborn. "No one's here. You're imagining things," he insisted.

Surprisingly, Shiomura's wife, Miwako, for once sided with him. "If someone's here, he'll call out," she said. For Miwako this Sunday was special because Shiomura had stayed home, probably on account of the rain shower; he usually played golf on Sunday. The family—Shiomura, Miwako, Mayumi, and eleven-year-old Mamoru—had just finished brunch. Their conversation was not out of the ordinary, but they all laughed frequently. Perhaps Miwako did not want to interrupt their merriment to go into the kitchen and check.

"Mayumi, your ears are out of tune," Shiomura said.

"Me? No way. You're the one with the bad ears. You're out of tune even when you laugh," she retorted.

"So laughter has a tune?"

"Sure, it does," Mayumi declared. Her plump face had given her the nickname "Shumai," after the Chinese-style dumplings. When she was serious her eyes showed more of their whites, just like her mother's. "If you don't believe me, go ahead and laugh, Daddy. You're the only one out of tune."

Shiomura began to laugh but then caught himself, saying he wouldn't want to laugh when there was nothing funny. Hearing this lame excuse, the other three burst into laughter. Even quiet Mamoru, who seldom laughed, joined in. The loudest and merriest voice of all belonged to Miwako, Shiomura's wife. Finally Shiomura laughed too. Though he knew very little about music, the laughter of his family on Sunday afternoon sounded better than the most splendid chorus.

There is an old saying in Japan that age forty-two is a man's most crucial year. So far Shiomura had been fortunate: his immediate superior had been promoted to managing director in the annual springtime personnel shifts; he was about to pay off the mortgage on their home; his blood pressure was normal and his stomach condition good; he was a fine golfer. "The snail's on the thorn: God's in his heaven—All's right with the world!" Was that Browning? Shiomura wondered. But he hadn't seen snails in the backyard for years.

"It's a thief," Mayumi whispered again, insisting that someone was in the kitchen. "He's just closed the door and left."

"You don't give up, do you, Mayumi?" Shiomura said. "Why not just go and have a look yourself?"

Miwako joined in. "There's nothing worth stealing in the kitchen. He'll be disappointed." Laughing, she headed for the kitchen. Peering inside, she uttered a cry of surprise and then looked back, puzzled.

"What's the matter? Anything stolen?" Shiomura asked her.

"Not stolen—added," she replied. On the earthen floor of the kitchen was a plastic bucket with a six-inch gray crucian carp swimming inside it.

"What is this?" shouted Shiomura. "Mamoru, did you do this? Did you make a bet or something with a friend?"

Mamoru looked at the fish and shook his head. Miwako and Mayumi had no idea why the fish was there either.

"Isn't this strange? How did it get here when no one knows anything about it? Did it walk up here by itself?" Shiomura's voice rose. Miwako, Mayumi, and Mamoru all looked blank.

"I know!" Miwako cried and turned to Shiomura. "It's you!"

Shiomura felt he had been hit by a hammer. "What's that supposed to mean?"

"Now just calm down. Put on your thinking cap a moment," his wife said.

Shiomura knew he was trembling.

"Have you been picking on someone who likes to fish?" she continued. "Saying things like he could never catch such a big fish or something? I bet that person got upset and deliberately left this big one he caught without telling you."

Shiomura was relieved. Good. She hasn't got wind of it. But I shouldn't relax yet, he thought. Making a long face, he said, "I don't have any friends who fish."

"No? So, you don't know who did it?"

"How could I know? Don't be silly." Shiomura's voice grew unusually loud.

"I sometimes hear about 10,000-yen notes being left in mailboxes, but I've never heard of a carp in a bucket," Miwako said. Looking at Shiomura with an eerie, cautious expression, she asked, "Don't you think we should report this to the police?"

"What could the police do? It's not money, you know,"

Shiomura said. He did not want the matter to go to the police. He doubted it was the sort of thing to be reported in the newspapers, but he certainly didn't want the police involved.

"But Daddy, it's a lost and found case, isn't it? It's not right to keep the fish for ourselves." Mayumi had been argumentative lately.

"It may be lost, but there's been trespassing here." Shiomura responded with another argument. No police, for God's sake, he thought.

"It's only a fish. Don't exaggerate, dear," Miwako laughed.

His wife's laughter gave Shiomura some relief. "Go get rid of it somewhere," he said to Mamoru. Just as he was reaching in his pockets to offer him a tiny bribe, the boy, who had had his fingers in the bucket and been playing with the fish, asked if he could keep it. Clinging to the bucket, he promised to give up on the pair of roller skates he had been asking for. Normally a very quiet boy, once Mamoru spoke up he would not back down. Shiomura had never permitted Mamoru to keep dogs, cats, or pigeons because he didn't want the house to get dirty, but he couldn't think of any reason not to keep the fish. Mayumi didn't want it because she didn't like the way it had gotten there. Miwako looked confused, not knowing what to say. Mamoru held the bucket tightly and in the end won: he would keep the fish.

Left alone—the other three had gone to search the shed for a bigger container for the carp—Shiomura heaved a big sigh. No doubt about it. This one is Mr. Carp. Not that I remember its face, but I recognize the rear fin, the way it's torn in the center. Has he grown this big and fat in the year I haven't seen him? But why would she do this?

The woman's name was Tsuyuko. Divorced, aged thirty-five, when Shiomura got to know her she was working in the

Ikebukuro section of Tokyo at a small Japanese-style restaurant owned by a relative. One night, after drinking too much, Shiomura had vomited on the floor and she had cleaned up after him. To show his thanks he bought her a handbag, and after seeing each other a few times, they became lovers. Gaunt and bony, Tsuyuko was not a beautiful woman. But even small things filled her with pleasure. Her conversation was just chitchat, never touching on sorrow or joy; these she was able to express in bed. Once she scratched Shiomura's back with her fingernails, and since it was summer he had had a hard time hiding the marks from his wife. Before he knew it, Shiomura had begun to visit Tsuyuko's apartment once a week. Around that time she began to keep the carp.

Tsuyuko had come across some children trying to throw a fish they had caught into a ditch full of dirty water. Letting the fish loose in soapsuds would kill it, she told the children, and asked them to give it to her. Then she bought a large tropical fish tank. She'd grown up in Kasumigaura in Chiba Prefecture, a fishing town, so she knew how to look after fish.

"I feel like he is watching us," Shiomura said. In Tsuyuko's cheap apartment with three- and six-mat rooms, the tank was just above their heads as they lay on their futon.

"Don't you worry. Fish are near-sighted," Tsuyuko said.

Shiomura was not sure that was true.

"I didn't mind living alone after my divorce," Tsuyuko said, "but now you've reminded me of what it is like to be with a man. When you don't come, I can't bear the loneliness unless I have something alive and moving in the room." Tsuyuko clung to Shiomura, like a morning glory wrapping itself around a bamboo stalk.

She named the fish Mr. Carp and fed him grains of cooked rice from time to time.

It wasn't that Shiomura came to dislike Tsuyuko or that even the small amounts of money he gave her seemed too extravagant. The real reason he left her was that he did not want to break up his family. He was not unhappy with his wife. At least, that was not why he had had the affair with Tsuyuko. When he went to Singapore on business for a month and then spent the following month in bed with colitis, he took advantage of this natural interruption to stop seeing her. A year had now passed. Shiomura told himself many times that he had never made Tsuyuko any promises about the future, and that she had no reason to hate him for leaving. Now, just when the memories were receding, Tsuyuko had left him Mr. Carp.

What was Tsuyuko's message in this? Was it a sign that she was angry, or a kind of revenge? He knew he could call her to ask, but he lacked the confidence that he would not fall into the abyss again. At any rate, Tsuyuko must have heard them all laughing. A married couple and two children. Merrily laughing together. How had Tsuyuko taken that?

I don't want to keep this fish, Shiomura thought. I should have made some excuse when Mamoru started begging for it. But I can't change my mind now; it will seem strange. It's not good to make them suspicious. Mamoru is just a boy. Boys get bored with things quickly. I'll just wait and then let it go free the first chance I get.

The fish had no facial expression. His round eyes looked as if they had been cut from black vinyl and pasted in, like the eyes on the paper carp pennants used for Boy's Day in May. The profile was dignified but from the front the fish looked exactly like former Prime Minister Shigeru Yoshida. There was guile in the way the face revealed nothing. The fish's mouth gulped and closed. Shiomura stared at the fish from the front and thought he had actually caught its eye, but nowhere in the black vinyl did it register "Ah, it's you" or "Oh, it's been a long time." Perhaps the fish had no memory of Shiomura. There was no way to determine what Tsuyuko's intention was.

That Sunday passed with a great fuss made over the carp. They could not find a container large enough for the fish, so Mamoru got an advance on his allowance from his mother, ran to a goldfish shop in the neighborhood, and bought a large, square water tank for 3,500 yen. The shopkeeper told him he should not use water right out of the tap; either he had to let the tap water sit for at least a half- to a full day in the sun or he should add in some chemical dechlorinator. As instructed, Mamoru ran water into the tank, threw in two bean-size tablets of dechlorinator, stirred, and dropped in the fish. Once in the water, the carp relieved itself, producing a surprisingly large stool—it was about the thickness of a pencil as it emerged.

"Mr. Carp, you've got some nerve," Shiomura muttered, thinking no one was around.

"Oh, you've named it Mr. Carp?" his wife asked, standing behind him. Shiomura was horrified.

They put the tank with Mr. Carp on top of the shoe shelf in the entryway. The quiet middle-aged woman who collected for the *Asahi* newspaper rang the front bell timidly and spoke in a small voice. In contrast, the collector for the *Yomiuri* newspaper had a booming voice and would press the bell as if to break it. Mr. Carp had a bad reaction to the loud *Yomiuri* collector, jumping violently and splashing water all over the entryway. It was easy enough to mop up the water, but spots remained on the teak-paneled door frame and walls, perhaps from the dechlorinator. The contractor had suggested plywood when the house was being built, but Shiomura had insisted on the importance of the entryway and spent quite a lot of money for genuine teak wood. Although he knew this was not Tsuyuko's way of getting her revenge, he still couldn't control his anger. He sensed his blood pressure rising.

The fish required looking after. An abundance of excrement and left-over particles of rotted fish food quickly made the water murky and turbid. In the dirty water, Mr. Carp would pucker its lips and knock against the four corners of the tank, inhaling and exhaling small bubbles, seemingly desperate for oxygen. And it didn't like the convenient ready-made food, preferring the kind you crushed in your fingers, but this soon dispersed and dirtied up the water.

Mamoru studied a book he had bought entitled *All About Carp Fishing.* "Mr. Carp is our relative," he said, shocking Shiomura. Listening to his son's explanation, Shiomura realized it was so. Fish are vertebrates, with fins instead of legs. From an evolutionary standpoint, humans are closer to fish than to some four-legged land creatures because the roots of mankind lie in the ancestors of the vertebrates on land.

In light of this, the face of Mr. Carp seemed that of a very deep thinker. "I know it all," it seemed to say. Mr. Carp knew, for example, that Shiomura had taken pains so as not to be embarrassed at karaoke bars: he had bought a book of lyrics to popular songs and, with Tsuyuko as his teacher, had practiced Aki Yashiro's famous "Boat Song." Mr. Carp had also seen Shiomura stark naked after a bath, pretending to do Tai-chi to make Tsuyuko laugh and then grabbing her and moving onto the bed.

What helped Shiomura was that his wife, Miwako, was so unruffled. At first, she had seemed preoccupied with the fish, but after a few days, she didn't talk about it much. She could just as easily have been taking care of a plain goldfish bought at some festival. Mayumi, however, detested Mr. Carp. She grum-

bled that the house had stunk of fish ever since it arrived. Averting her face, she refused even to look at the fish. Instead, she
stared insolently at Shiomura.

As long as Shiomura was away at work during the day he
was fine, but at home, sitting in the family room, he would suc-
cumb to nervous exhaustion. Mealtimes with the family were
the worst. Inevitably his eyes would stray to the fish tank, which
was now right next to the TV. How could he possibly relax? It
wasn't simply like having a pet; it was like having someone new
added to the family. No wonder the right side of his neck—on
the same side as the tank in the room—had developed a cramp.

Massaging his neck, Miwako asked, "Shall I move the
tank?"

"No. It's got nothing to do with the tank," Shiomura said.

"Really? But you keep watching it all the time," she said.
She pressed the painful spot on his neck so hard that he
screamed and jumped up.

The beer had lost its flavor, and Shiomura didn't much feel
like going home. He still couldn't read anything in Mr. Carp's
black vinyl eyes. Nor was there anything he could tell from
Miwako's brown goggle-eyed expression. As for Tsuyuko,
watching from God knows where, he had absolutely no way of
knowing what she was thinking.

The Sunday after Mr. Carp arrived, Shiomura asked
Mamoru to go for a walk with him. "You don't mind just wander-
ing around places you've never been to, do you?"

"No, that's okay," Mamoru replied.

Shiomura said nothing more, and in silence the two took a
bus from Ikebukuro, getting off at Shiinamachi, where Tsuyuko
lived. Shiomura could not explain his actions, even to himself.

He knew well enough what it meant to take his own son to the neighborhood where his ex-mistress's apartment was, but he couldn't help himself.

Mamoru followed Shiomura, as usual without a word. They walked past the supermarket, the greengrocer's, and the fish shop. From the tea shop next to the kimono shop, the fragrance of roasting tea leaves floated in the air, just as it had a year ago. Tormented, Shiomura felt the salt being rubbed into his wounds. He moved down the street to the lane where Tsuyuko's apartment was located, the same place he had come some forty or fifty times before. What would he say to Tsuyuko if she came out from the apartment and ran into them?

Some of the residents of Tsuyuko's apartment house had gotten to know Shiomura during the year he had come visiting her. To avoid encountering them now, Shiomura walked around the side of the building. Tsuyuko's apartment was the second window from the end on the second floor. She must have moved out, for the clothes hanging at the window were those of a young couple with a baby. Shiomura noticed that Mamoru too was staring at Tsuyuko's window with him. Realizing he had been caught, Mamoru quickly turned his face away, without saying a word.

This is as far as I should go, Shiomura thought. But still he felt like torturing himself a bit more. He wanted to take his son, who had taken over the care of Mr. Carp, to visit all of his and Tsuyuko's old haunts—partly out of a sense of duty to the boy but also to help atone for his poor treatment of Tsuyuko.

Shiomura entered a coffee shop two buildings down from the public bathhouse. He and Tsuyuko always used to drop by the shop on their way back from the bathhouse. The owner of the shop, a man about sixty years old, was sitting in his usual place and wearing his usual expression, a horse-racing newspaper spread in front of him. When he saw Shiomura, he waved in welcome and began to speak, but noticing Mamoru behind he lowered his hand and kept silent. Shiomura sat in the very place he had sat in with Tsuyuko and spoke to Mamoru loudly, so the owner of the coffee shop could hear him: "I'll have coffee; what do you want, Mamoru?"

"A soda," Mamoru said.

The startled shop owner looked sharply at Shiomura. This had been Tsuyuko's usual order.

Father and son drank their coffee and soda in silence. Pretending to read his paper, the shop owner shot occasional glances at them.

"I wonder how things are . . . ," Shiomura said as he paid the bill. He omitted "with her," but the shop owner seemed to understand.

"Doing well, I guess," he said.

How had Tsuyuko spent her days during the year since he had stopped coming to see her? Did she have a man she could go to the bathhouse with, and did she then stop in at the coffee shop and have a soda? Shiomura wanted to know, but the shop owner had lowered his eyes to his paper after returning Shiomura's change. Shiomura could guess from his expression that Tsuyuko didn't hate him too much. So that was that. He couldn't help how things had turned out. When Tsuyuko had moved out of her apartment, she must have had a slight grudge, so she had slipped in and dropped off Mr. Carp, the idea being that Shiomura should look after him for her from now on. A self-serving interpretation to be sure, but Shiomura chose to believe it. A person good at keeping herself happy should be good at managing her sorrows as well.

I will take good care of Mr. Carp, Shiomura vowed. I'll treat him well so he lives a long long time, but if I can't I'll take him to Kasumigaura and let him go. Kasumigaura was Tsuyuko's hometown, and Shiomura thought that if it did come time to let Mr. Carp go, he would just take Mamoru with him and leave his wife and daughter behind.

Mamoru did not speak at all on their way home. Once, when Mamoru was about five, Shiomura had taken him to a baseball game. When they returned home, Miwako had asked, "Mamoru, where did you go with Daddy?"

"Television," he had replied.

This had become a family legend, but what would the boy say today? Shiomura wondered. When Mamoru spoke, Shiomura expected his wound to smart again.

Lost in such thoughts Shiomura arrived home to find Mr. Carp floating belly up in the fish tank.

"Soon after you two left he stuck his mouth up above the water and started gasping for breath. Then he turned on his side and just stopped moving his mouth," Miwako said. Not knowing what to do, she had left the fish there until they returned.

Mamoru stared at his mother in disbelief as she explained what had happened. Mr. Carp was floating with his big round eyes open—the eyes of a paper carp pennant. He appeared to be doing a casual back float. His fan-shaped scales still held the color of the sunset.

Just then Shiomura noticed that the sound of the piano had stopped. Mayumi was standing beside him. "Carp don't make any noise when they die, do they?" she said. "I thought it would suffer a lot, splashing water all over, but it didn't at all."

"Well, he didn't leave a will either, did he?" Shiomura said, trying to sound calm, and let out a giggle. He felt sorry for Mr. Carp, but the feeling that at long last he was freed from Tsuyuko was stronger than his pity. For a moment, he imagined that Tsuyuko had drowned herself and that her body was floating somewhere in the sea off Kasumigaura. But this notion was just the product of his male conceit. He pushed it aside.

"Mom, you didn't put detergent or anything in the tank, did you?" said Mamoru.

"What? What did you say? What makes you think I would do such a thing? Don't be silly!" Miwako's goggle-eyes rolled up, revealing her triangular whites. Immediately her tone of voice returned to normal and she asked, "Mamoru, where did you go with your dad?"

Mamoru did not reply to that. In silence, he put his hand into the tank and poked at the fish. The fish was no longer a fish; it had become something else, floating and bobbing on its side.

"Mamoru, where did you go with your dad?" Miwako demanded.

Mamoru gently poked at the fish and pushed it down into the water again. "Bow wow!" he said, barking like a dog.

Ears

THE WATER IN THE ICE BAG MADE A SLOSHING SOUND UNDER his ears. The ice inside had already melted and, with every move of his head, the sound of the lukewarm water, lapping like waves against a boat, vibrated his eardrums. My temperature has gone down, Kusu thought. He knew that if he got up and went to work, he could still make it to the afternoon meeting, but he decided against it. It's not bad to take a day off once a year. Never being late or absent was a way of getting ahead a decade ago, but nowadays such a boss is regarded as strait-laced and commands little respect from his subordinates. Sniffing the rubbery bag, which smelled as if it had been left to dry in the sun, Kusu felt the need to behave like a spoiled, weak child.

He remembered playing hooky in elementary school. The thermometer seemed to stay under his armpit forever. His mother read the temperature with grave concern. Unless the mercury went above 37° Centigrade, he would have to get up and go to school. Viewed from his bed, his mother's face looked childish, cute. She must have been washing something, for her hands were wet and puffy. She wore an apron of white calico and for some reason had placed several rubber bands around her wrists.

In a corner of the room, a kettle steamed on a large ceramic brazier. Whenever Kusu caught a cold, his mother cooked Chinese oranges with sugar—she said it was good for his throat—

and the sweet-and-sour smell spread all over the house. She pressed her cold palm on his forehead to check his temperature. Sometimes she pressed her forehead to his, tickling his nose with her breath and the smell of her hair oil. Once the water from the ice bag had leaked out, perhaps because the fastener was bad, and the water had wet Kusu's ears and neck. His father, fretting over the danger of an ear infection, had his wife put the boy into flannel pajamas that had been warmed up near the floor heater. Kusu recalled how jealous he was of his father, who would command his mother only on such occasions.

The tepid water in the ice bag sent up noises under Kusu's earlobes. The peaceful sound and the smell of rubber were nostalgic, but Kusu felt strangely uneasy.

It was Shinjiro, Kusu's younger brother, who had gotten the ear infection. Some roads have signs that say "Dead End." There are also small shacks, barely large enough for a man, with signs reading "Danger!" or "Do not touch" in red. His younger brother's ear infection had meant "Dead End" or "Danger!" on the road ahead for Kusu. Having gone so far, and without understanding why, he had had to stop, turn right around, and come back.

Kusu sat up on his futon. He couldn't just keep listening to the leisurely slosh of the water. "Hey," he called out to his wife. But then he remembered he had told her he was taking the day off and would take care of the house for her. So she had gone out. Kusu put his wife's half-kimono robe around his shoulders and walked to the kitchen for a glass of water. The house looked different minus the family. The small two-story home with five rooms was suddenly vacant and cold.

In the kitchen, Kusu found himself looking inside the open refrigerator. This was before turning on the tap water, although he had no intention of eating. Why am I doing this? He laughed at himself, but from the refrigerator his hand automatically moved to the cupboard drawers, which he pulled out one by one from the top down to check their contents. Receipts from the dry cleaner and the liquor shop, rubber bands, candles, an empty eyedropper, and matches were all in a jumble.

Kusu turned next to the family room. He told himself it was shameful to search the house when no one was around, but he still wanted to open the big futon closet and the drawers in his wife's dressing table to see what was inside. As he suppressed the temptation, he realized he was breathing hard.

A married couple with a son and a daughter, Kusu and his wife were just an ordinary family with no particular secrets. Kusu had never dreamed of poking through the house while everyone was out. He had never got into such a habit. He had been married almost a quarter of a century without even once opening his wife's handbag.

What has happened to me? Do I still have a fever?

As Kusu sat alone in the parlor, all the walls and closets in the house seemed in collusion, as if hiding something from him. Something small boiled up inside him. If he remained there any longer, he felt he would open the closet or run upstairs to his daughter's room to check her wardrobe or desk drawers. He felt unsettled. Smoking would help at a time like this, he thought, and he regretted that he had, with immense difficulty, quit smoking six months ago.

By examining various items through the magnifying glass he used when checking a word in the dictionary, Kusu was for a while able to suppress his urge to search the house. Even fingernails have rough edges when viewed up close. And the skin on one's hand looks like the small pointy waves of the sea as seen from an airplane. Where a tatami mat is worn or frayed, what looks like the core of a millet husk is exposed, and each grain becomes a small cushion. Kusu was moved by his discovery of this ordinary detail.

He found a fluffy lump of lint most interesting. The sleeve of his wife's half-kimono robe was partly turned up. He turned the sleeve down, picked off some lint, laid it on the dining table, and looked it over. The lump was rounded like the sleeve and appeared to be made up of thin, soft felt, but when Kusu inspected it through the magnifying glass he saw it was actually a collection of fibers of various colors. Several hairs entwined around a tiny silver-colored breath mint and a red silk thread were bent in the shape of a half-moon. The whole thing looked so fragile that it might break into pieces if lifted. The gray lump was like a flower that had blossomed on earth by mistake.

Kusu wondered if this was what the *udumbara* flower looked like. The *udumbara* is a legendary Indian flower that blooms only once in every three thousand years and can be an omen of both luck and doom. Looking like a gray fluffy cloud, or a bird's nest, the lint was like the petals of the flower, and the silver breath mint and red silk thread inside it were the stamen and pistil.

Kusu had forgotten both her name and face. All he remembered was that the little girl was two or three years younger than he and that she had lived in the house next door to him for a brief time—six months to a year. No, no. That wasn't all. He remembered something else clearly: she had a red silk thread hanging from her ear. There was a wart the size of a grain of rice on the small projection just inside her ear, and the red silk thread was tied around its base.

"When it's tied tight, the wart will slowly rot and fall off," she said, showing her ear to Kusu.

"When I finish my bath, my grandma ties it with a new

thread. It needs to be tied more tightly, but that hurts. Daddy told grandma to tie it gently. So this wart won't come off for a long time." The red colored silk thread swayed in the air.

Kusu had just entered first grade; he watched the girl's dangling silk thread across the low hedge that separated their yards.

"Daddy always puts me on his lap and pulls the thread on my ear. He shouldn't be doing that." The little girl bounced a small handball, making the red silk sway again. The thread was tied up in an elaborate feminine way and looked like an earring.

Kusu observed the little girl's ear. It looked like a small snail. What a strange shape ears have! You have one on the right and on the left, each with the same shape. If you took them off and put them together, they would fit together perfectly, like two shells. He wanted to touch the girl's ears. He wanted to pull the red silk thread hard to make her say, "Ouch!" He wanted her to cry. Though the thread was not tied hard, the little projection that had at first looked like a white grain of rice gradually changed its color and became a silver berry. Kusu wanted to put the berry in his mouth and bite on it gently. And he wanted to look at the girl's face at that very moment. He wanted to peep inside the hole just above the berry. What was deep inside her ear?

"Don't you dare touch your ear!" Was it before or after his mother shrieked that she slapped him? Kusu often touched his ear, but why did his mother get so upset and hit him only on that one occasion? Was it because his younger brother, Shinjiro, had gone to the hospital with an ear infection? Shinjiro's bandage for his ear went around his head. The boys' mother told the neighbors that water had gotten into Shinjiro's ear while he had been splashing and playing. That's what she told Kusu too. Or had that been a dream?

It was a fine, clear day, and no adults were in the house. Kusu took a large box of matches from the kitchen into the hall-way, for he wanted to look into the neighbor girl's ear. A little before then, the bath in his house wasn't working and he had gone to a local bathhouse with his father. Just before going inside, Kusu had dropped the coin he was clutching, which was to pay for his bath, into a ditch. His father pulled out a box of matches, struck one, and held it over the ground. There Kusu saw the coin glinting at the bottom of the murky water that smelled of sulfur and floating soap scum.

Kusu struck a match and moved it close to the girl's ear, but it was still too dark to see clearly. He struck another match and moved it closer in. I should be careful not to burn the silk thread. Cautiously he moved the match even nearer the hole. Then suddenly the flame was swallowed up into the darkness. Shinjiro screamed and began to cry, and the red flame went out. Why did Shinjiro cry? Why he, instead of the girl?

Kusu flung open the futon closet doors in the dining room with both hands. He grabbed anything he could reach and tossed it into the air. Then he pulled out all the drawers from the chest and the dressing table and dumped their contents onto the floor. Hot, thick emotion shot up inside him. If he did not keep his body in motion, animal-like groans leaked from his mouth.

Shinjiro was nicknamed "Victor" for the spotted black-and-white dog that was the trademark of an American record compa-ny. Shinjiro was hard of hearing in one ear, so when listening to people or music he would turn his good ear to where the sounds were coming from, thus assuming the same posture as the dog. Kusu couldn't recall what grade Shinjiro had been in, but on a new notebook Shinjiro had signed his name "Victor Kusu." The whole family had had a good laugh at that, but then their laughing mother had suddenly pushed away the laughing Kusu, held Shinjiro tightly, and begun to cry. Squeezed in her arms, Shinjiro had squirmed and wriggled. "What are you doing? You're hurting me!"

Had those words been directed at his older brother?

"Victor's" ear problem subtly affected his future. He made a point of not applying to top-ranked universities or companies. He became taciturn and stubborn. He was unlucky in love, and he was almost forty before he got married. His wife dragged one leg slightly when she walked.

Kusu ran upstairs, entered his son's room, and pulled open the desk drawers. Out came the pornographic magazines. Then Kusu grabbed the Walkman headphone from the bookshelf and flung it to the floor. Next he flew into his daughter's room. As he tugged on the desk drawers, he felt a sharp pain on the bottom of his foot. There was a piece of gold jewelry about the size of a tack head attached to a rod. Immediately Kusu recognized it as a pierced earring.

Just two weeks before, he discovered that his daughter had gotten her ears pierced. They had argued about it at dinner.

"It's in style now. Everyone has it done," his daughter defended herself.

"If you do what everyone does, will you also steal or murder if everyone else does? Is that what you're saying?" Harsh words were exchanged and neither yielded. The two refused to speak to each other for a few days.

"Shouting won't fill up the hole once it's made. I guess times have changed." His wife made peace between them.

The bleeding and the pain enraged Kusu. He pulled open the desk drawer and found a woman's lighter, and then a pack of cigarettes farther back. He put a cigarette in his mouth and lit it. His hand was visibly shaking. Perhaps because he had not smoked for six months or still had a fever, he felt giddy. He ransacked another drawer; she had a stylish ashtray. Kusu kept puffing on the cigarette. It was slightly damp, and the smoke made his eyes tear up.

"Daddy, what are you doing in here?" His daughter's voice took him by surprise. She had just come home from the university. "You have no right to come in here without asking. Even if you're my father you have no right!"

The next thing he knew, Kusu had slapped her. "How dare you say that? What is this for?" he said. He shoved toward her the cigarette he had been smoking and a lighter, then raised his foot to show the mark the pierced earring had made. He knew he was not making much sense.

Kusu's wife returned soon after and defended him in their daughter's presence, though she was shocked by the chaos in the house. "Besides your cold, you have high blood pressure or something, don't you?" she asked, looking into his eyes.

The ice bag, stuffed with crushed ice, made squeaking sounds under his ears. The edges of the ice crushed and creaked against each other, fighting without yielding. The sun-dried smell of the rubber was gone; all that remained was the piercing numbness of his ear from the cold.

Both Kusu's parents had passed away some time before, so there was no one he could ask about what had happened with the match flame. He thought of visiting Shinjiro, whom he had not seen in four or five years, and he counted the days he could take off with pay. His younger brother lived far up north in Hokkaido, where he operated a small cheese factory. Even if they were to get together, Kusu knew he would sit drinking in silence in front of the wood stove, while his brother would adopt his "Victor" posture and, in silence, look at the snow outside the window. It never hurt to try. He should ask his brother about the little girl next door with the red silk thread. Shinjiro was only four then. Kusu knew his brother would probably just tilt his head, incline his body, and say, "I don't remember her." What would I say to that? Kusu wondered, but his head, numbed by the ice, froze the words together with the decades that had passed and nothing came out.

Half-Moon

HIDEKO WAS STILL AFRAID TO LOOK AT THE CHARACTER FOR the word "finger," though it had been almost a year since the incident. Whenever she opened up a newspaper or a magazine, the character would jump out at her, looking different and larger than the others on the page. What people said about your heart aching was true: at such times she would feel a pain wringing her chest, and she would sweat lightly. Then when she looked more closely, she realized it was usually not the character for "finger" standing alone but a combination of that character with others in words like "appointment," "instruction," or "specification," and she was relieved.

The character for "finger" was not all she was afraid of: she dreaded seeing first graders, and in particular, boys. Whenever she saw a boy with a brand-new cap on his head and a leather school bag on his back, holding his mother's hand, she imagined it was Kenta. Not wanting to look at the boy yet unable not to look, Hideko felt the pain in the center of her heart reappear.

Kenta was the son she had left with her husband when they separated. At the start of the school term in spring, she could avoid the television commercials showing "brand-new first graders" by turning her face away, but when she ran into real first graders on the road, she could not ignore them. She made her living selling cosmetics door to door, so she had to go out. Yet she could not walk looking up at the sky; there was something she wouldn't want to see there either.

It was on their way back home after Hideko and her husband, Shuichi, had ordered their wedding rings that they saw the moon in the daytime. Shuichi had just bought a pack of cigarettes as they were leaving the department store near the Sukiya Bridge in Ginza. "Look, there's the moon!" Hideko cried, pointing up at the sky.

"Don't be silly. The moon comes out at night," Shuichi said, putting his change into his coin purse, which was designed in the shape of a football. He looked upward. "It's true! It's daylight but the moon is out," he said in quiet astonishment.

Hideko was amazed. In almost thirty years, had he never seen the moon in the daytime?

"I've kept my nose to the grindstone instead. I've never had time to look up at the sky during the day," Shuichi explained. He had lost his father when he was a small boy and been raised by his mother. He had held all the part-time jobs one could name. He had gotten through university by attending evening classes and working during the day.

Hideko gripped Shuichi's hand that still held his wallet. She felt her emotions well up from deep inside. The two stood still for a while among the bustling crowd on the Sukiya Bridge. Later, looking back, she remembered that moment as her happiest moment ever.

The transparent white half-moon floated in the pale blue sky above the skyline. "Doesn't the moon look like a fat white radish? Like a miscut thin radish slice?" Hideko asked Shuichi.

Hideko's grandmother had been skilled with her hands. Though her knuckles were thick, her fingers were especially supple, and she performed all the customary women's chores, such as sewing and washing kimono and repapering the shoji screens. Because her ability to handle a kitchen knife was a source of special pride to her, she often spoke ill of her daughter-in-law, Hideko's mother. "That woman has beri-beri of the hands," she would carp. In late December, as New Year's approached, she would assign Hideko's mother the end-of-the-year housecleaning and take over all the cooking, busying herself with making ricecakes for the New Year's Day feast. She would sit little Hideko beside her on a thin rush mat in the cold, old-fashioned kitchen and demonstrate her adeptness at peeling and slicing white radishes for *namasu*, a radish and carrot salad.

First a round radish had to be sliced as thin as a sheet of paper. After demonstrating how to do this difficult job, the grandmother would hand Hideko the vegetable knife. But Hideko's radish slices always turned out either too thick or lopped-off and shaped like a half-moon. When her grandmother saw Hideko's work, she would say that the girl had inherited her mother's "beri-beri hand." Perhaps Hideko did not like to hear her mother being spoken ill of, for she learned to hurriedly pop the miscut half-moon radish slices into her mouth before her grandmother could see them. Now, as an adult, when slicing radishes Hideko was still in the habit of eating her mistakes as soon as she made them.

Hideko told Shuichi this story at a coffee shop in Yurakucho in Ginza.

"Wow," Shuichi whispered several times, each time shaking his head as if to say no—his habit whenever he was moved or in a good mood. At the same time, he turned his football-shaped coin purse upside down on the table and sorted the change inside into hundred-yen and ten-yen coins. Every time he bought something, even a small item such as a pack of cigarettes, he would obsessively record the purchase in his pocket notebook and then sort out his change on the spot. Such stinginess was unseemly, thought Hideko at first, but when Shuichi told her about his boyhood, she understood.

His mother sold insurance, and it was Shuichi's job to do all the shopping and prepare the dinner. His mother was meticulous, and fussed over a loss of even ten yen, so Shuichi had developed this habit of counting his money. Hideko could imagine the boy Shuichi sitting at the dinner table, licking the tip of his pencil, recording the day's expenditures—"eighty yen for four potato croquettes"—on the back of an advertising flier.

"Wow," Shuichi repeated, stirring the coffee in his cup, having finished the sorting of his coins. "Tell me more."

So Hideko told him that, thanks to her grandmother's teaching, she still sharpened her kitchen knives every night before she went to bed and a ten-yen coin was the best thing to use when sharpening a knife.

"How do you use it?" Shuichi asked her.

Taking one of the ten-yen coins from his purse, Hideko gave Shuichi a demonstration, letting a long narrow menu serve as the knife. She explained that the most important thing when sharpening a knife is the angle of the blade to the whetstone. But that's hard for amateurs to maintain. So if you slip a ten-yen coin between the back of the blade and the stone you can use the resulting angle and get a well-honed knife every time.

"Wow." Shuichi shook his head again and returned the coin to his purse.

Shuichi retold this story to his mother that evening over dinner after announcing that he and Hideko had ordered their wedding rings. His mother had called for some sushi from a nearby shop, and although she listened intently her face barely moved.

"Ever since my husband passed away, I have been so very

busy," she said, gesturing as if using an abacus, "and I haven't cooked much. But, come to think of it, it would be easier for a bride not to have a good cook as a mother-in-law. Don't you agree?" With a deft smile no doubt cultivated in her insurance business, she added, "Too sharp a knife is said to be bad for even an unborn baby."

Shuichi's mother was fifty-eight years old, but with her dyed hair she looked five or six years younger. Hideko had not wanted to live with her, but had been talked into it with the promise that the money Shuichi's mother earned selling insurance would be used to pay off the mortgage on their new house.

Kenta was born half a year after their wedding. "Eldest son born. 3,170 grams. Perfect condition. *Banzai!*" Shuichi wrote on a large sheet of shoji paper that he posted on the wall. He did not take it down even when Hideko returned from the hospital. Smearing Kenta's palms and the soles of his feet with black ink he made hand and foot prints on fancy rice paper. Shuichi said doing this every year would make a good keepsake for Kenta. His boss at work did the same thing at his house. Shuichi was like an excited child.

The years passed with no outstanding problems, though Hideko and Shuichi had the usual petty quarrels of any marriage. Soon the fancy papers with Kenta's hand and foot prints numbered six, and the boy's hand, which looked like a black maple leaf, had doubled in size.

One clear day after the rainy season was over, when Hideko was pregnant with her second child, she went to a hospital early in the morning to learn that the baby's foot-first position had returned to normal. Relieved, she made her way back home, and to celebrate the good news she stopped at a toy shop along the way to buy a monster mask that Kenta had long been asking for.

Her mother-in-law had put their clothes out to air before leaving for work, taking advantage of the good weather after the long rainy season. Her kimonos and Shuichi's suits, hanging in the living room and on the clothesline in the backyard, exuded the smell of mothballs. Kenta ran among the clothes, wearing the new mask and imitating a voice he had learned from a monster movie on television.

In the kitchen, Hideko was slicing a ham she had received as a mid-summer gift. Not every night, but every three days or so, she made it a practice to sharpen the kitchen knife using a ten-yen coin. Her happy mood was reflected in the way she sliced the ham as thin as possible.

"Boowahh!" Kenta dashed into the kitchen, screaming like a monster, and stretched his hand out across the cutting board. He liked the end of ham and had decided that the piece was his.

"Be careful!" Hideko cried out, her hand slipping, making a half-moon slice. As she automatically put the miscut slice into her mouth, Kenta reached his hand out once again.

"Watch out!" Hideko meant to utter, but her mouth was stuffed with ham and her voice didn't come out. She felt resistance to the knife and then saw a tip of Kenta's forefinger, three-quarters of an inch long, lying at the end of the cutting board.

Kenta's finger could not be put back. Their house was located in a new suburb, so the ambulance was horribly slow in coming. Unwilling to wait and ignoring Hideko's attempt to stop her, Shuichi's mother picked up Kenta and ran off to a doctor's office in the neighborhood. But the doctor was not there, and while she was dashing off to yet another clinic, the ambulance finally came. Perhaps because of all the delays in obtaining treatment, or because of Kenta's own constitution, the operation did not go well.

Shuichi rushed to the hospital. He did not utter a word to Hideko, who bowed her head to him—a tacit gesture of apology—and sat at Kenta's bedside. Sedated, Kenta slept with his thickly bandaged right hand lying up beside his head as if he were raising his arm to ask a question.

"You're not a chef. An amateur like you doesn't have to sharpen your knife every night," said Hideko's mother-in-law. "When my child got wild or bratty, I never ever had a knife out or used hot oil for tempura. I was criticized for always buying prepared foods and take-out meals, but look at him! My son is over thirty and has never had a single injury or burn!"

Hideko looked at her husband, waiting for him to say, "That's enough. It's useless to say things like that now. Don't you see? Hideko feels it the worst. And it's partly Kenta's fault; he romped around and got his hand in the way." But Shuichi held Kenta's left hand and remained silent.

Kenta left the hospital in three days, just as Hideko was admitted: the shock of the accident had caused a miscarriage. She did not lament the loss of the baby; in fact, she thought it was best. If the baby had come, she would have been kept busy by it, with little time left for Kenta. She would have had to hold the baby to feed him, but it was Kenta that she wanted to apologize to by cradling him in her arms.

By the time Hideko returned home from the hospital a week later, Kenta had become his grandmother's pet. Holding his bandaged right hand to his chest, he went behind his grandmother as if to hide, and not once did he utter the word "Mama." That was bad enough, but when Hideko went to the kitchen for a glass of water and saw a new knife in the knife rack, she was shaken. "Mother," she blurted out "my knife . . ."

"I switched it."

"What do you mean 'switched it'? Do you mean you threw it away?"

"You just stay out of there for a while." Her mother-in-law meant that Hideko should not use a knife, that she would handle the work in the kitchen herself. To emphasize her message, on the table for dinner that evening she placed ready-to-eat food in plastic trays from the supermarket.

Hideko's mother-in-law stopped selling insurance. She said it was because of Kenta, but the truth was that her arthritis had gotten worse and walking was becoming a struggle.

Kenta's bandage was removed and Hideko's health had improved, but Shuichi did not touch his wife. Once he stretched his arm out toward her after turning off the light, but he quickly withdrew it. Neither his heart nor his body forgave Hideko; you couldn't just sort things out into piles of ten- and hundred-yen coins.

Hideko began to work part-time in the early fall. She said it was to earn money for the mortgage, but the real reason was that she could not bear to face her mother-in-law every day in the small house.

"What did Kenta do with his hand?" asked a little girl, one of her son's playmates, around the time Hideko began going to her job. Standing behind Hideko was her mother-in-law, and behind her was Kenta.

"I munched it down because Ken-chan was so-o-o cute and I love him so-o-o much," Hideko told the girl.

Her mother-in-law almost carried Kenta away into the house, slamming the door behind her.

Christmas decorations were starting to appear on the city streets. An end-of-the-year party was scheduled at the company

where Hideko worked. The party took place after hours, and
Hideko knew she would be home late, but since Shuichi was
away on a business trip and she did not want to be stuck at
home knitting with her mother-in-law in the family room, she
decided to go. After the party, she went out for more drinks and
didn't get back until almost midnight. Her mother-in-law would
be in, so Hideko had not carried her housekey. She rang the bell
at the door to the home, but no one came out. She pressed the
bell several times, calling out in a low voice for fear of waking
the neighbors. When there was still no response, she went
around the house and knocked on the back door, but the door
remained closed.

A half-year later, Hideko had a new job and a new apartment, and was separated from her husband. In order to sever any
lingering attachment she made a point of finding flaws in
Shuichi's character. You could be nice and call him scrupulous,
but in fact what he was was petty. Whenever he was given a box
of cakes individually wrapped, for instance, he would immediately open it, count out the pieces, and distribute them: "Four
for Kenta; three for grandmother; two for Mama; one for me."
Or, when he came home from work, he would record all the
money he had spent that day before even changing his clothes.
Once he asked Hideko to give him ten yen. When she asked
him why, he said his accounts did not tally; he was feeling so ill
about it that he wanted to make up the difference from the
household money.

Hideko told herself that she could never entrust her life to a
man who did not blame her for the accident but also did not
defend her to his mother. She hated her mother-in-law, who was
now taking revenge on Hideko for stealing her only son. And
Kenta. How the grandmother had brainwashed him, she did not

know, but ever since the accident Kenta had stopped being Hideko's little boy.

It doesn't matter. I don't care, Hideko told herself. Before long, the character for "finger" won't upset me anymore.

In early summer, when the new first graders began to look like ordinary elementary school pupils, Hideko received a phone call from Shuichi. Guessing that he wanted her to sign the divorce papers, she went to the coffee shop where they had agreed to meet.

Shuichi did not have the papers. "I was asked to come in to Kenta's school," he said. Kenta had been telling stories to explain the accident whenever his classmates teased him about his short forefinger: "My hand got caught in the door of a sports car." "My pet tortoise snapped at me." "My grandma chopped it off with a knife." When Hideko heard that Kenta had not blamed his own mother, tears rolled down her cheeks. Shuichi pushed his handkerchief toward Hideko in silence. It was gray and dirty. He must have been using it for many days.

When they left the coffee shop, Shuichi took hold of Hideko's wrist tightly and started walking without a word. He led her to a nearby love hotel. It had been a year, and when the surge came over her, Hideko shed hot tears once again. "Come back to us, please," Shuichi said as he parted from her, getting on the bus.

Hideko walked slowly through the town that fine, clear afternoon. What shall I do? Should I go back? To the place that matters most and the place I hate the most?

Hideko decided she would go back to her family if the moon was there in the daytime sky. But when she tried to lift up her eyes, fear of what she might not see kept her from looking. She walked on, disregarding the sweat that trickled down her back.

The Window

EGUCHI HAD NOT KNOWN THAT EVERY HOUSE HAD ITS OWN face that aged over time. Then, in the fall personnel changes, he was transferred to one of his company's slower departments. The nightly banquets and parties after work suddenly stopped, and he was able to see what his own house looked like at dusk. It looked exhausted: the stone gate and mortar walls were covered in a white powder, and after years of exposure to wind and rain the large wooden nameplate, a gift from a senior executive who thought highly of his own calligraphy, looked like an old beat-up sandal. Fifteen years before, when Eguchi had had the house built, this executive had been his biggest booster at work. But after using Eguchi up, he had moved him into a sinecure, much as if he were retiring a worn-out shoe. In order to accommodate the fine nameplate—his tiny house was only nine hundred square feet and his plot of land was barely twice that size—Eguchi had spent beyond his means to plant a pine tree at the gate. The pine was now more brown than green.

When he was at his old job, Eguchi had dashed out early in the morning and come home late at night, delivered by limousine right to the gate. On Sundays he would play golf or sleep in. So he had rarely had an opportunity to take a good look at his house. Its beaten-down appearance reflected his own.

An evening paper was sticking out of the mail slot beside

the gate. Before he was demoted, this sort of thing had never happened. Mitsuko, his wife, in a rare act of diligence, would pick up the paper just as soon as it was delivered and lay it on the dining table with her husband's eyeglasses. Now he was being taken lightly at home as well as at work. Indignant, he yanked the newspaper out of the mail slot. For a brief moment, glancing up at a small window on the second floor of the house, Eguchi thought he saw his mother, Taka, who had died five years earlier, looking down at him through the narrow panes of glass. But it was his married daughter, Ritsuko. Seeing him, she gave Eguchi a limp salute. Her gesture reminded him of the *pan-pan* women—prostitutes for the Allied soldiers—who saluted in jest to the Americans.

Ritsuko looked like Taka. The vague, thin eyebrows; the watery eyes with bags under them; the small mouth opening as if to say, "Ah"—everything resembled Taka. If Ritsuko were to wear her hair in a pompadour, she would be an exact double of Taka when she was young. Ritsuko was beginning more and more to resemble the very last person Eguchi wanted her to resemble. Stepping into the entryway, he had a sense of foreboding. Had Ritsuko come home for the same reason Taka had?

"Flea couple." Eguchi remembered checking this phrase after getting a dictionary as a present when he entered middle school. When he was younger he had heard his parents described as a "flea couple," and he was disheartened to read in the dictionary that it was true—the male flea was smaller than the female. His father was thin and frail. His mother, Taka, was taller only because of her puffed-up hairdo, although she did have an ample frame. A rude relative was said to have sneeringly described them, in their now discolored wedding photo, as a broom and a straw rice bag. His father, wearing a creased A-line kimono skirt, appeared to be leaning on his bride, who wore a white wedding kimono with a white bride's hood. Eguchi remembered the broom that hung beside the kitchen door, and how it swung every time the door opened.

Eguchi's father was something of a milquetoast. Taka always carried the heavy bundles when they went out; at night, as it got colder and windy, Taka would take off her muffler and put it around her husband's neck. In the summer his father always had stomach problems; in the winter he caught cold. After returning home from work, he had to take oxygen before going to bed. With the inhaler placed on the low dining table, Taka would test the temperature first with her own mouth, lest there be burning steam, and wrap her husband's neck with a towel. As Eguchi's father inhaled vapor, a white dew would collect around his mouth, making him look all the more pitiful.

His father was sensitive to cold, but Taka was just the opposite. Complaining that her feet were warm, she would leave them outside the futon even in winter. In contrast, his father often slept in long underwear made of camel hair. When Eguchi went to the kitchen at night for a glass of water, he could hear the live clams for the morning's miso soup making sounds in a basin. The clam shells were slightly open, and from some of them poked the tip of white tube, exactly what for he did not know. Taka's foot, sticking out from under the brown futon, was just like that white tube. Some of the clams, perhaps surprised by noise, squirted water. There might be a rusty knife in the basin, too, since the metallic flavor was supposed to make the clams disgorge their sand. Whenever Eguchi saw the clams and knife in the basin, or Taka's protruding feet, he felt himself tingle.

His mother loved fresh water and gulped it down in large glasses, throwing her head back and making noise with every swallow. His father claimed that fresh water gave him diarrhea;

on rare occasions, he would have his wife boil him some water, which he would then drink from a teacup the size of a sake cup. His mother always had beads of sweat along her hairline, but his father would seldom sweat except at night. As a child, Eguchi often wondered why a man and woman so different from each other had married. When he asked his mother, she said, "It's better to mix things up, I guess." Then she smiled. "Unless you have variety, you won't have healthy children."

Eguchi couldn't remember whether his mother had made this comment before or after he went with her to the town of Ashikaga in Tochigi Prefecture. She had grown up the daughter of a large textile dyer there.

"She didn't bring Kenichi with her?" Eguchi asked his wife. He had expected to see his grandson's small shoes next to Ritsuko's, but there was only a single pair. Mitsuko, who came to the entrance to greet Eguchi, shook her head slightly and pointed upstairs. She probably meant to say that Ritsuko had come by herself. Mitsuko was never a talkative woman, but the stiff way she shook her head and her gesture warning him not to let Ritsuko overhear confirmed his fears.

"Has anything happened to her?" he asked.

Mitsuko put her finger to her mouth. "Later," she whispered, then quickly added, "Please don't ask her any questions."

Ritsuko came downstairs, her slippers tip-tapping. "It's early, isn't it? Did you come straight home at five, Dad?"

"Your father's been on time every day since he joined the General Affairs Section," Mitsuko said.

How cruel of this woman, thought Eguchi. She, who had never even worked in an office, had blurted out the very last thing he wanted anyone to say.

"Then, there's no point bringing a cloth sack at the end of

the year, is there?" Ritsuko said, referring to the excess of end-of-the-year gifts that had piled up in the alcove when Eguchi was a manager.

"Bring a paper bag this year," Eguchi joked back. His eyes spied Ritsuko's overnight bag in a corner of the dining room. He was right; she had come home to spend the night.

The two women went into the kitchen and chatted as they prepared dinner.

It had been a large rattan basket that time for sure. Holding onto Taka's hand, Eguchi had got on the train or a streetcar, probably the Tobu Line, as they headed for Ashikaga. Taka was carrying the large basket, and that windy winter evening she had hidden her face in a deep red velvet shawl. Eguchi liked riding on trains and sat at the window as usual, but he could not see anything outside because it was so dark.

"Why didn't Daddy come with us?" Though at the time only five or six years old, the boy Eguchi knew he shouldn't be asking this question. He suspected that this trip was on account of Toku-san, an office boy at his father's company who was putting himself through night school. Heavy framed and taciturn, he could probably have beat anyone else at the company in a wrestling match. Because of his strength Toku-san had been instructed to come to Eguchi's house to help Taka by putting up shelves and cleaning the house, garden, and chimney. At noon, he sat on the wooden veranda and ate his lunch from a large aluminum lunchbox. Eguchi had seen his mother, as she served tea to Toku-san, suddenly stretch out her hand to pick up a piece of his lunch and put it in her mouth. He was startled.

Back then, Eguchi had one of those indoor swings for children that could be hung from a door frame and looked like a box made of woven cane and wood. The arms and the back were upholstered with a red-flowered artificial silk material, which he didn't care for because it made it look like the swing was for a girl. Eguchi, like his father, often caught cold, and was seldom allowed to go outside to play. So Toku-san would push him in the swing. Eguchi liked him, since he pushed the swing harder than his parents did.

One day when Toku-san was at the home, he gave the swing a push and then went to a room in the back of the house with Eguchi's mother, leaving the boy alone in the dining room. The swing came to a stop, but Toku-san did not come out to push it again. Eguchi got off the swing and pushed it himself. The box with red silk flowers swayed by itself in the dimly lit room. It was probably after this that his mother took him back to Ashikaga.

In Ashikaga, Eguchi came down with infant dysentery. The futon he slept on there was strange: a patchwork of sample dye swatches of gray and navy blue. In the night he awakened to find his father, who had just come up from Tokyo, dashing toward Taka and almost leaping up to slap her in the face. When Eguchi woke later, it was still the middle of the night, but his father was on his knees, apologizing. He had no recollection of anything else, except that Toku-san stopped coming to their house.

Eguchi had been formally introduced to Mitsuko as a potential marriage partner, and he had decided on her because she was the complete opposite of his mother. "She looks like a burdock," said Taka, laughing disrespectfully on their way back from their first meeting. Compared to the ample, fair-skinned Taka, Mitsuko was indeed a burdock, lanky and dark.

Eguchi liked Mitsuko because she carried herself as if she knew she was not much to look at. She may not be interesting to live with, but at least she won't betray me, he thought. He did not want to spend his life like his father, proud of his pretty wife and at the same time eaten away by jealousy. People did not call Mitsuko a "pretty housewife"; they called her "unassuming" or "rock steady." And Eguchi was content with these descriptions.

A girl was born the second year of their marriage. "She takes after her grandmother," people said. This frightened Eguchi. Genes really did reappear over generations: Ritsuko's fair skin, her chubbiness, her thirst for water, and her tendency to perspire—all resembled Taka.

When the little girl was about three years old, Eguchi walked into the dining room after a bath to find Ritsuko pressing her face to the television. "Ugh! Don't lick that!" he said, and then suddenly realized she was kissing an actor on the screen.

By the time he came to his senses, his daughter was on the floor, screaming and crying. Pushing Mitsuko away as she tried to stop him, he hit Ritsuko again and then again. That night, he recalled, he confessed to his wife about his mother.

As she grew older, Ritsuko came to look even more like Taka. Whenever Eguchi heard her described as "a pretty daughter" he felt joy and pain at the same time. Whenever Ritsuko put on heavy make-up or made a brightly colored dress for herself, or whenever her male friends called her on the phone, Eguchi's expression turned blatantly sullen. Immediately after her coming-of-age ceremony at age twenty, Ritsuko's engagement was set, and Eguchi was more relieved than Mitsuko, partly because his future son-in-law was so good-looking. This one is all right, he thought.

Taka passed away around the time the wedding date was decided. The death was sudden and unexpected. Taka's sickly husband had passed away seven years earlier, but Taka had looked ten years younger than her real age and was in good health. One day she went shopping and took a bus back home. When the bus reached the end of the line, Taka did not wake up. The conductor shook her, only to discover she was dead. She had suffered a heart attack. In her shopping bag they found a necktie in department-store wrapping paper, and at the wake the conversation turned to speculation as to whom the necktie was intended for. "I think she bought it for Ritsuko's bridegroom. She liked young, good-looking men," said Eguchi's wife, and the rest agreed. But Eguchi did not think so.

Taka had always needed a Toku-san or someone like him; she couldn't live without one. After Toku-san had stopped coming to the home, Eguchi once glimpsed Taka looking out from the small sealed window on the second floor just above the stairway. Taka stood before it for a long time, pressing herself against its glass. From the window the grounds of the high school in front of the house were in clear view. Perhaps Taka was watching the high school students doing their exercises. Eguchi himself had seen them exercising, naked from the waist up.

It was after this that Eguchi's father had fallen from the roof. He injured his hip and had to take a long sick leave from his company. Was the accident caused by his climbing up on the roof to board over the window? Through its glass he must have seen Taka's dim, tearful eyes; the vague, thin eyebrows; and the ah-shaped lips. The hip injury caused him constant pain in the winter; he aged, and as he aged he shriveled.

Mitsuko had suggested that he take the necktie for himself as a keepsake. Unable to get this episode out of his mind, Eguchi insisted, against his wife's wishes, on placing the mysterious necktie inside Taka's coffin, to be cremated with her.

The dinner that night saw more food and conversation than usual, but Eguchi's heart was heavy. He was concerned about

Ritsuko, yet he was forbidden to ask questions. Although his wife knew how he felt, she ignored him and kept making small talk. He didn't like her doing that. Only I know why she came home, Mitsuko seemed to be saying, and this obviously gave her some sort of feeble maternal pleasure. The secretive glances his wife sent his way and the cheery topics she deliberately chose further got on his nerves.

Don't be so pretentious. Why don't you just tell me? Sooner or later I'm going to find out. Besides, I can guess what happened. Eguchi suppressed what he wanted to say and finished the dinner.

As she began to peel fruit for dessert, Mitsuko suddenly pressed her hand to her chest and slumped forward. She had a chronic gallstone problem, and it wasn't bad enough to call for an ambulance, but it had begun to rain and Eguchi feared that getting a doctor would not be easy. Mitsuko, now doubled over in pain, told him the phone number of the clinic. "If you tell them it's me, the younger doctor, the son, will come."

The "younger" doctor was actually over forty, but he was in very good shape and nicely tanned, probably from playing golf so often. He jumped out of his car, dashed into the house without an umbrella, and strode into the room where Mitsuko was lying, without waiting to be ushered in. His speed and assurance indicated he had been to Eguchi's house many times and knew it well.

As Mitsuko exposed her chest for the doctor to examine, Eguchi and Ritsuko waited in the adjacent dining room. Eguchi sensed a sweetness and coquetry in Mitsuko's voice that he had never heard before as she explained her pain to the doctor. He barely controlled his urge to open the sliding-door partition and burst into the room.

That night, Eguchi was betrayed a second time. Ritsuko was drinking water in the kitchen, when Eguchi, also thirsty, came in. "Well, Daddy, I think I should tell you, too." She rinsed the glass in running water, shook it twice to drain the water, and returned it to the dish rack, just as she used to do when she was living at home, "Apparently, there . . . there's another woman."

Eguchi began to giggle. "Ho ho!" A huge surge of laughter he could not suppress welled up inside him.

"What's so funny?" Ritsuko pouted. In profile she looked exactly like Taka.

Eguchi kept the rest of his laughter to himself. He felt sorry for his daughter, but he assured himself that everything now would be all right. Things were turning out just the way they're supposed to. His son-in-law would be the one to avenge his father. Filling the glass Ritsuko had just put down, Eguchi thought how surprised he had been to glimpse an aspect of a woman he had never known before in Mitsuko's sweet voice as she spoke to the doctor (though he was sure there was nothing going on between them). He heaved a deep sigh at his mistaken assumptions about Ritsuko, too, and wondered which episodes among the several he could recall about Taka had the deeper significance. He realized he had been as much in love with Taka as his father had.

Instead of boarding up that window, I think I'll replace that old nameplate out front with a new one, even if my calligraphy is bad, Eguchi thought. He sipped his water slowly.

Afterword

ON AUGUST 22, 1981, A CHINESE AIRPLANE HEADING FROM TAIPEI to Kaohsiung crashed, leaving no survivors. On board were several Japanese passengers, including the writer Kuniko Mukoda. The media coverage of Mukoda's unexpected death was intense, and the subsequent "Mukoda boom" in Japan attested to the tremendous popularity she enjoyed at the time. Her emergence as a writer and her sudden exit from this world at the peak of her maturity and productivity was compared to the path of a comet.

Kuniko Mukoda was born in Tokyo in 1929 to a self-made insurance company executive. She was the eldest daughter of four children. After graduating from Jissen Women's College with a degree in Japanese literature, she worked for several years as an editor for a foreign movie magazine. Mukoda also wrote radio scripts on the side to help support her hobbies, which included skiing, mountaineering, and traveling. When the demand for her radio work increased, Mukoda turned to it full-time. In all she produced over a thousand scripts. With the advent of television, she began to write teleplays, and by the 1970s she had become one of the most sought-after scriptwriters in Japan.

In 1976, Mukoda contributed short essays to *Ginza Hyakuten*, a monthly periodical. A collection of these essays, *Letter of Apology from Father* (*Chichi no Wabijo*), was published in 1978. In this book she related her experiences at home, at the schools she attended, and in various towns she had lived in as her father was transferred from place to place. The book provided an excellent picture of prewar middle-class family life in Japan and established Mukoda's reputation as an essayist.

At the urging of her friends, Mukoda began to write short stories for the monthly periodical *Shosetsu Shincho*. These were published from February 1980 to February 1981, and for the first three of them—"The Name of the Flower," "The Otter," and "I Doubt It"—Mukoda was awarded the prestigious Naoki Prize for Popular Fiction. When the serialization was completed, the thirteen stories were published in book form under the title *Cards in Reminiscence* (*Omoide Toranpu*).

Ten of the works in this collection ("The Otter," "The Name of the Flower," "I Doubt It," "The Doghouse," "Small Change," "Beef Shoulder," "Manhattan," "The Window," "Half-Moon" and "Ears")

1.456 y

are from *Cards in Reminiscence*. "The Fake Egg," "Mr. Carp," and "Triangular Chop" are from *Fortunate and Unfortunate Times* (*Odoki, Medoki*), which was posthumously published in 1985.

The Nobel Prize–winning author Yasunari Kawabata commented once that Japanese women writers reveal more of themselves in their works than men writers do, and that this tendency can be found even among those women writers who ostensibly did not write about their own lives and personal experiences. Kuniko Mukoda, a discreet individual with a prewar middle-class Tokyo upbringing and demeanor, did unconsciously expose some of her more eccentric proclivities in her work. (Had she lived to realize this, she no doubt would have been mortified.) Partially this was the result of working in the pressure cooker that is show business in Japan. In a single day, for example, she used to complete, by herself, an entire script for an hour-length television drama. Always pressed by deadlines, she had no time for revisions and tended to repeat herself. The hands of her male characters were often described in great and similar detail, for example, revealing one of Mukoda's more pronounced fetishes. I have taken the liberty of eliminating some of the more incidental of these passages when it was possible to do so without distorting Mukoda's original text. I have also made some minor alterations to reduce redundancy. Naturally, all responsibility for the translation lies with me.

It should be said in Mukoda's defense that her radio and television scripts no doubt made her particularly adept at pacing and structure, and at inserting small but telling details in her written work. Her stories often ended with an ironic twist or a cleverly worded sentence. These elements, along with Mukoda's impressive renderings of modern Japanese families and of men and women confronting their lack of mutual understanding, are very much in evidence in this collection.

Among the translations here, "I Doubt It" first appeared in the Summer 1984 issue of *Japan Quarterly*. "Small Change" first appeared in the Summer 1989 issue of *Meanjin*, a literary quarterly published by the University of Melbourne. Further minor revisions have been made to both works for this collection, and I am grateful to both publishers for their permission to include them here.

Tomone Matsumoto
Terre Haute, Indiana